Fear at the Festival

Also by Gordon Snell

Fear at the Festival

GORDON SNELL

POOLBEG
FOR CHILDREN

Published 2001
by Poolbeg Press Ltd.
123 Grange Hill, Baldoyle
Dublin 13, Ireland
Email: poolbeg@poolbeg.com
www.poolbeg.com

©Gordon Snell 2001

The moral right of the author has been asserted.

Copyright for typesetting, layout, design ©Poolbeg Group Services Ltd.

1 3 5 7 9 10 8 6 4 2

A catalogue record for this book is available from the British Library.

ISBN 1 84223 109 X

Cover design by Steven Hope
Typeset by Patricia Hope in Stone Serif 10/15
Printed by Cox & Wyman

About the Author

Gordon Snell is a well-known scriptwriter and author of books for children and adults. Other books in the series include *Dangerous Treasure, The Mystery of Monk Island, The Curse of Werewolf Castle, The Phantom Horseman, The Case of the Mystery Graves, The Secret of the Circus and The Library Ghost.* He is also the author of *The Tex and Sheelagh Omnibus.* He lives in Dalkey, Co. Dublin, and is married to the writer Maeve Binchy.

For dearest Maeve, with all my love.

1

Festival Plans

"Tina, Tina! Stop that!" cried Molly. "You bad dog, come here!"

Molly ran into a lane which led off the main street of Ballygandon, down towards the fields and the river. There were some black plastic bags of rubbish dumped there, and Tina had ripped a hole in the side of one of them and was burrowing inside, snuffling happily.

Brendan and Dessy followed and dragged the dog away, while Molly got Tina's lead out of her anorak pocket and clipped it to her collar. Tina began to bark as Molly pulled her along and they came back into the main street.

"She must have found something tasty in there," said Brendan.

"Maybe she thought it was a doggy-bag take-away," said Dessy.

Brendan was Molly's cousin, and he and their friend Dessy were here staying with Molly and her family for the summer holidays. They called themselves The Ballygandon Gang, and they had had many adventures together. They liked to think of themselves as Private Eyes, solving mysteries and bringing villains to justice.

"If the people in Ballygandon go on dumping their rubbish like that," said Brendan, "you'll never win the Tidy Towns competition, that's for sure."

Molly wasn't going to let her home town be slagged like that. She snapped: "I suppose the streets round where you live in Dublin are as clean as Switzerland!"

"Oh, Brendan's out there with his vacuum cleaner every morning," said Dessy. "Hey, I've got an idea. Why don't we start an *Untidy* Towns Competition? We could ask everyone to dump their black bags in the street, and throw away their burger cartons and drinks cans wherever they like."

"People do that already," said Brendan. "We'd need something dramatic, like daubing all the houses with mud."

"Or spilling a truck load of manure into the road," Dessy suggested. "You country people would be easy winners there. We're a bit short of manure in Dublin."

"You're a great help, you two," said Molly. "I can just imagine people flocking into Ballygandon for the Untidy Towns Festival."

"A festival!" said Brendan. "That's an idea. It would liven up the town all right. Lots of other places have them, why not Ballygandon?"

"What kind of a festival?" asked Molly.

"Well, there are all kinds," said Brendan. "Tralee has the Roses, and Wexford has operas."

"A Joke Festival would be no good," said Dessy. "I'd win all the prizes."

"Yes, and have all the audiences running for cover," said Molly.

"Let's go and take a look in the library," said Brendan. "There should be books there which would give us some ideas."

"Good thinking, Brendan," said Dessy.

* * *

They went into the old stone library building. The librarian, Joan Bright, was at the counter, checking some library cards. She was a lively woman, small and round, with wavy ginger hair and large pink glasses, and she always encouraged young people to use the library.

"Hello there," she said, "I was going to contact you today. There's an e-mail for you, from your film-star friend in Hollywood."

"Billy Bantam!" said Molly.

"That's right. I've printed it out for you." She handed Molly a sheet of paper.

They had made friends with Billy when he came to Ballygandon to film *The Curse of Werewolf Castle,* and he had even brought them over to California for a holiday.

"Is he coming to see us?" asked Brendan, looking over Molly's shoulder as she read.

"Not just now," said Molly. "He's letting us know that his new movie is having a premiere in Ireland soon, and he says he can get us tickets."

3

"Great!" said Dessy. "Roll out the red carpet. I'll just *have* to buy me a new dinner jacket!"

"I'll bring my camera and take pictures of the stars as they step out of their limousines," said Brendan.

"What's the film called?" asked Dessy.

"Terror in Toyland," said Molly. "Billy plays a child vampire."

"Not much make-up needed there, then!" Dessy laughed.

"Can we e-mail him back?" Molly asked.

"Of course, you can," said Joan Bright, "but there's someone using the computer at the moment. While you wait, have a look round and see if there are any books you want to take out."

"As a matter of fact, there's something we came to ask you about," said Brendan.

"Ask away."

They told her about their idea for a Ballygandon Festival, and how they wondered what sort of events it should have. Joan Bright was enthusiastic.

"Yes, a festival. That would really be a big attraction for the town. Now let me see. I have some calendars of events in Ireland, and books about putting on shows, and organising events. Then there's one about pageants, I remember." She began to scurry about the bookshelves, picking out books.

"What's a pageant?" asked Dessy, as the three of them followed her round the library, taking the books from her.

"It's a kind of procession, with people dressed up in costume, and performers and bands. It usually marks some anniversary, a religious one sometimes, or else a big local event in history."

4

"Sounds great to me," said Molly. "I could play my tin whistle."

"I'll dress up as a clown and walk on stilts," said Brendan, "and Dessy can coil himself up inside a tractor tyre, and be the *Human Yo-yo*."

"Thanks a lot," said Dessy. "I'd prefer to be a Human Cannonball, and aim myself straight at *you!*"

"Let's put all the books here," said Joan Bright, going across to a table in the middle of the library. They spread the books out and began to leaf through them.

"Wow!" said Brendan suddenly. "That's quite a show!" He pointed at a picture of a huge parade going down a street. There were dancers with flared skirts, drummers and trumpeters, brightly dressed girls with feather headdresses waving from carts pulled along by plumed horses, and people wearing giant grotesque masks of clowns and devils and queens and kings.

Molly read the caption underneath the picture: "Mardi Gras carnival in Brazil."

"A lot of South American and West Indian countries have carnivals like that," said Joan Bright. "Mardi Gras means Fat Tuesday, when you eat as much as you can before giving things up for Lent."

"That sounds good to me," said Dessy, taking out a bag of toffees.

"Not in the library please, Dessy," said Joan Bright. Glumly, Dessy put the bag back in his pocket.

"A procession like that would blow their minds in Ballygandon!" said Brendan.

"It might be a little bit ambitious for a small place like

5

ours," said Joan Bright. "But there's no reason why we couldn't have a procession of some kind."

"We'll get everyone to make costumes and masks," said Molly.

"And borrow some donkey carts," said Brendan. "And maybe your dad would lend us his pick-up truck."

"Maybe," said Molly doubtfully.

"A festival should have other events going on as well," said Joan Bright. "What about some traditional music and dancing?"

"Fantastic!" cried Molly. She got out her tin whistle and began to play a jig. Dessy started to dance. Then they saw Joan Bright frowning, and stopped.

"You'll disturb other people in the library," she said. They looked around. The only other person there just now seemed to be a man in the far corner, beside the local history section.

He had very short black hair and a trim moustache, and was dressed in a smart blue jacket and check trousers. He was about forty. He was looking up from the book in his hand, and smiling at them.

"Sorry," said Joan Bright. "We got carried away."

The man raised his hand and said: "No problem, ma'am." He had a slight American accent, Brendan thought, as they turned back to the books.

Joan Bright whispered: "That's the man who was using the computer. When we've sorted out a few more things for the festival programme, you can go and e-mail your friend."

They suggested all kinds of events, some exciting, and some plain ridiculous.

"What about a race around the town?"

"And a speed rock-climb up to the ruined castle!"

"A ghost-hunt there in the middle of the night!"

"A marathon step-dancing contest!"

"Face-painting!"

"A tug-of-war!"

"A fishing competition on the river!"

"And raft-racing too!"

"A yo-yo contest!"

"A flour-throwing match!"

"Hold on, hold on, I'm trying to write all these suggestions down," said Joan Bright. "There certainly should be enough to choose from there. With the pageant, of course. Now if we could find some historical event to celebrate, that would give the whole festival a focus."

"What about Princess Ethna's wedding in the castle, hundreds of years ago?" said Molly.

"That's a bit gloomy, isn't it?" said Brendan. "She was murdered the night before."

"And her ghost haunts the castle," said Dessy. "Maybe she'd join the procession!"

"I have an idea," said Joan Bright, "but I'll have to look up a history book. Why don't you go and send your e-mail?"

The three of them went off to the computer room. Sleeping on the keyboard was the library cat, a big fluffy black creature with white paws. She was called Internet, because she used to spend so much time sleeping in the computer room. When they came in she opened her yellow eyes and gave a *miaow* of greeting.

"We'll have to move you, Internet," said Molly, picking up the cat and placing her on the desk beside the machine. Internet settled down and went straight back to sleep.

"I've got Billy's e-mail address in my notebook somewhere," said Brendan, sitting at the keyboard.

"Hey, why don't we ask Billy over for the festival?" said Molly. "He'd be a star attraction."

"Especially if he wears his vampire costume," Dessy laughed.

They sent the e-mail, saying they'd love to go to the film premiere, and telling him about the festival they were planning.

Back in the library, they saw Miss Bright standing with a book open, and looking excited.

"I believe I've got the answer!" she said. "Look at this. Over two hundred years ago, the Earl of Dunslaggin made a ceremonial visit to Ballygandon, to confer a knighthood on the local landlord, Horace O'Toole. Horace wanted to put on a big show for him, so he hired fancy costumes and masks for all the people to parade in. But he was so arrogant and harsh that the people hated him. They pretended to go along with the plan, but just as the Earl was about to knight Horace with his sword, the crowd began to shout and jeer, and they all surged forward and swamped Horace, knocking him down and then throwing him in the pond. The Earl was very angry."

"I bet Horace was, too!" Brendan exclaimed.

"He certainly was, but because everyone was in costume and disguised, they could never find out who the main rioters were. The Earl rode away in disgust, declaring

8

Ballygandon an outlaw town never to be mentioned in any report or given any goods that were being distributed to the poor rural areas. He even tried to get the town's name removed from the maps."

"The Ballygandon Revolution!" said Molly, raising her fist.

"Up the rebels!" cried Brendan, doing likewise.

Dessy raised his too and said: "Horace O'Toole, you're a great big fool!"

"I think we can use Molly's words," said Joan Bright. "The Ballygandon Revolution. It's worth having a festival to mark that. What's more, the exact date when it happened is in exactly six weeks' time. August the twenty-fifth. It's a bit short notice . . ."

"We can do it, Miss Bright!" said Molly. "We'll get busy right away, getting things ready."

"Now I don't want to be downbeat about it," said Joan Bright, "but we are going to have to think of how we'll raise some funds. We shall need a certain amount of money to stage things like this."

"Excuse me," said a voice nearby. It was the man in the blue coat. "I couldn't help overhearing what you were talking about. I think a festival is a great idea."

"Thank you," said Joan Bright. "It was these young people's idea, in fact."

"Then they're bright kids," said the man. "By the way, my name is Barry Farrell. I'm from this part of the world originally, but I emigrated to the States nearly twenty years ago. Now I'm back to settle down."

"Well, you'll be welcome to come to the festival, Mr Farrell," said Joan Bright.

9

FEAR AT THE FESTIVAL

"Maybe you'd take part in it," said Dessy. "Are you any good with a yo-yo?"

"I'm afraid not. But in the States I was a promoter, organising shows and concerts and so on. I'd be happy to help you, and I might even be able to raise some money to help out too."

"Wonderful!" said Brendan.

"Thank you again," said Joan Bright. "Look, I have to close the library soon, and go home to see to my mother. Could you call in tomorrow morning, say about eleven, and we can talk about it then?"

"Sure, ma'am, I'd be delighted," said Barry Farrell. "See you then."

* * *

As they walked back to Molly's house for tea, the Ballygandon Gang talked excitedly about the festival.

"I'll be the Earl of Dunslaggin," said Brendan. "I can just see myself in a fancy cloak, waving a sword around and knighting people."

"I'll be the leader of the rebels," said Molly, "and Dessy can be Horace O'Toole."

"Not me," said Dessy, "I could easily get away from a pathetic bunch like you lot."

"Up the Ballygandon Revolution!" shouted Molly, and they all ran down the road, waving their fists in the air.

2

Rivals

When they got home, they were pleased to find that Molly's grandfather, Locky, was going to have tea with them. He was a tall, sprightly man with grey curly hair, who lived at a retired people's home called Horseshoe House. He was always happy to join in any escapade, and he'd been with the Ballygandon Gang on several of their adventures.

They were helping Molly's mother set the table for tea, when Brendan whispered to Molly: "Hey, you know Miss Bright was talking about getting funds for the festival? Well, do you think . . .?" he looked over towards the armchair where Locky was sitting reading a racing paper. He was always studying form, and betting on the horses, and sometimes he got very lucky.

"We could always ask," said Molly.

Locky looked up from his paper. "What are you two whispering about?" he asked. "Cooking up some devilment, as usual?"

"No, Grandpa, something exciting," said Molly.

"A festival," said Brendan.

"You're not starting to organise race-meetings already, at *your* age?" Locky pretended to look shocked.

"Of course not," said Molly.

Dessy chipped in: "Though come to think of it, that mightn't be a bad idea. We could have a horse-race through the streets of Ballygandon."

"Shut up, Dessie," said Brendan. "This is serious."

They sat at the table and told Locky about their plans for the Ballygandon Festival, and about the pageant and the story of Horace O'Toole.

"That sounds like your cup of tea, Dad," said Molly's mother to Locky. "You were always one for clowning around."

"What do you mean, clowning?" Locky replied. "I'll have you know, I was quite a good actor in my younger days. I'd always fancied myself as an Earl."

"You'd be great," said Molly. "There's just one problem about the whole thing. Miss Bright says we're going to have to raise some money . . ."

Locky shook his head. "I'd love to help you, but unfortunately the horses I've backed recently have all decided on a go-slow policy. Sorry."

"We'll just have to see what that Barry Farrell guy comes up with tomorrow," said Dessy.

* * *

But next morning, on their way out through the Donovans' shop, they got some unwelcome news. Mrs O'Rourke was at the counter, ordering things from Molly's father. She was a bossy, middle-aged woman who kept horses and caravans which she hired out to holidaymakers.

The Ballygandon Gang had had a number of battles with *her* in the past, and exposed various shady dealings she'd been involved in.

"Now let me see," Mrs O'Rourke was saying, "I'll need two sliced pans, a pound of rashers, two big cartons of milk . . ."

As he put the goods on the counter, Molly's father said: "A big order this week, Mrs O'Rourke."

"Yes, I have a lodger staying with me at the moment. And you'd better get ready to order a good deal of provisions in a few weeks' time, Mr Donovan. Think of all the people who'll be flocking into Ballygandon for the festival."

"Indeed," said Molly's father. "It will be a great boost for the town."

Molly and the others stopped at the door. Molly whispered: "How did *she* hear about it?"

Mrs O'Rourke said: "Of course, we'll have to make sure it's run properly, and with the right kinds of events. We can decide all that at the meeting tomorrow night."

Molly asked: "What meeting's that, Mrs O'Rourke?"

"The one I've just called. I put up a notice on the board of the community hall. Everyone's welcome to put their views."

"But we've already decided on a lot of things, with Miss Bright," said Brendan.

Mrs O'Rourke sniffed. "Very nice of you, but we couldn't let a bunch of kids run a festival like this. It's far too important. And as for that librarian, she couldn't organise a game of musical chairs."

They looked at her in rage, and Molly stepped forward, about to shout at her. Brendan held her back, and whispered: "Hold it. We'll only make things worse. Let's go."

He went out of the door, and Molly and Dessy followed. Outside, Molly exploded: "That woman! She's a monster! Remember how she tried to steal that priceless book from the library? *And* sell that field that didn't belong to her?"

"Yes," said Brendan. "If she's trying to get her hands on the festival, she'll wreck it. We must find a way to stop her."

"How about assassination?" suggested Dessy. He put on his gangster imitation: "If you guys want her taken out, I'm your man."

"You're a great help, Dessy," said Molly. "Let's go to the library and see what Miss Bright says about it."

* * *

Joan Bright was worried. "I'd rather not have that woman sticking her nose into it," she said, "but I suppose she's entitled to call a meeting if she wants to. We'll just have to go there ourselves and explain it was your idea in the first place, and show people what we've planned. I'm sure everyone will be delighted."

"She's up to something. I know it," said Brendan.

"Maybe she wants to hijack the festival, and run it her own way," said Dessy.

"And to her own advantage, no doubt," said Molly. "If Mrs O'Rourke can find a way of making some money, she'll go for it."

Just then, Barry Farrell came in. He told them he'd heard

about the meeting, and he'd be happy if they wanted to announce that he was ready to help promote the festival.

"You like our plans for it, then?" asked Joan Bright.

"Certainly. I think they're excellent."

Molly said hesitantly: "It's just that . . . well, we're worried that someone else will try to muscle in on it." She thought it wiser not to mention Mrs O'Rourke by name.

Barry Farrell was reassuring. "Oh, I think everybody will be very enthusiastic. And anyway, if there *are* people who have other ideas, we can always take a vote at the meeting. You're bound to get most support, and then you can go ahead."

"That's right!" said Joan Bright. "We must just make sure we get our ideas across."

"Will you present them for us, Miss Bright?" asked Molly.

"Only if you'll be there to help me," the librarian smiled. "Here's to the Ballygandon Revolution!"

* * *

The community hall was crowded. There must have been well over two hundred people packed into it. They took up all the chairs, and some people were standing against the walls.

There was a stage at one end, with a long table with chairs behind it. At one side was a large easel, with a big sheet of paper pinned to it. Brendan had printed on it in large red capital letters the words: BALLYGANDON FESTIVAL.

Molly's mother and father were there, and so was Locky.

The Gang had asked the local guard, Emma Delaney, to be the chairperson to organise the meeting. That way, they thought, there would be fair play, if anybody tried to undermine their plans. At the moment Emma was standing below the stage, at the front of the hall. Joan Bright and the Ballygandon Gang were standing near the steps at the side of the hall, that led up on to the stage.

They saw Mrs O'Rourke sitting in the front row on the right. They still couldn't work out just what scheme she was hatching, but they realised it certainly couldn't be anything helpful.

Then Brendan pointed in her direction and whispered to the others: "Look who's there, sitting just behind Mrs O'Rourke."

They looked across the hall at a glowering bald-headed man. "That's all we need!" said Molly angrily. "It's Seamus Gallagher!"

He was a friend of Mrs O'Rourke who ran a pub in the nearby town of Killbreen, and he'd been a partner in a number of her shady dealings, as well as having some of his own.

The Ballygandon Gang had often come up against them, and usually managed to foil their plans in the end. No wonder when Seamus caught their eye he frowned and glared at them, his eyes under his bushy eyebrows full of a fierce hatred.

There was a din of excited chatter in the hall, as Emma Delaney climbed the three stairs that led on to the stage, and went to stand at the table behind the centre chair.

"Now, if we could have some quiet please . . ." Emma

said loudly. The chattering subsided, but there was still some muttering going on. Dessy put his fingers to his lips and gave a shrill, piercing whistle.

There was some laughter, then gradually the hall became silent. Emma glanced across and said: "Thank *you*, Dessy!" Then she went on: "And thank you all for coming to this meeting to hear about plans for what I'm sure could be an exciting event which will be of great benefit to our town. I call upon our librarian, Joan Bright, to outline her plans, with the help of the three young people who thought up the idea, Molly, Brendan and Dessy!"

Joan Bright went up on to the stage, followed by the Ballygandon Gang. She stood beside the easel, while the three members of the Gang lined up on the other side. There was applause from the audience. Joan Bright blushed and smiled. Molly and Brendan grinned sheepishly and shuffled from foot to foot, but Dessy stepped forward and bowed, giving a big sweep of his hand.

"Thank you all," said Joan Bright. "Now before I outline our plans for the festival, let me tell you a strange story about things that happened right here in Ballygandon, long ago."

She told them all about Horace O'Toole and the Earl of Dunslaggin and the way the people of Ballygandon had got their own back on their oppressors. She was a good storyteller – she had had plenty of practice at the regular storytelling sessions for children she held at the library. The audience in the hall listened intently, and at the end of the tale they clapped loudly.

Joan Bright explained that the plan was to stage a pageant re-enacting the Ballygandon Revolution, with a procession through the town. Then she said: "And now, Molly, would you like to display the other events we have in mind for the festival?"

Molly turned back the first sheet on the easel, to show underneath it in big letters, three of the events they had thought up:

TRADITIONAL MUSIC
IRISH DANCE CONTEST
TUG-OF-WAR

There was a murmur of interest and approval from the audience, which continued as Molly turned back further sheets with more events on them. At the end there was applause again.

Joan Bright said: "Of course, we would welcome any suggestions anybody in the audience might have."

People in the audience voiced their ideas:

"What about a gymnastics display?"

"A jazz concert?"

"Athletics races for the kids?"

Joan Bright wrote down the suggestions. There was a pause, and Emma Delaney said: "Thank you, Joan. Now if there are no more suggestions, I would like to introduce you to someone who has returned to Ballygandon from the USA, and has offered to help us . . ."

Barry Farrell had just climbed on to the stage, when a loud voice from the audience interrupted: "I have another suggestion – in fact a number of them!" It was Mrs O'Rourke, who stood up, facing the stage.

"Very well, Mrs O'Rourke," said Emma, not looking too pleased. She knew a lot about Mrs O'Rourke's past activities. "Perhaps you'd like to tell us."

"I certainly would!" Mrs O'Rourke went to the stairs and climbed on to the stage. She strode across in front of the table to the other side of the stage from where Joan Bright and the Ballygandon Gang were standing. She reached behind a curtain and wheeled out another easel. On the first sheet were the words: THE BALLYGANDON MONSTER BASH.

There were some chuckles from the audience, but Mrs O'Rourke frowned them down as she proclaimed: "Fellow townspeople, I believe Ballygandon deserves better than that list of ordinary events, however worthy they might be. I believe our town deserves something that will really put it on the map. Something like this!"

She turned over sheet after sheet, each with one event in capital letters:

> ROCK AND ROLL!
> DISCO!
> CASINO!
> MISS BALLYGANDON CONTEST!
> POKER COMPETITION!   .
> CONCERT WITH ROCK STAR RAVEN!

There were other events, equally brash and raucous, and finally Mrs O'Rourke said: "That, ladies and gentlemen, is *my* plan to put Ballygandon on the map and into the twenty-first century!"

There was some scattered clapping, and a lot of muttering as people took in these proposals.

Emma Delaney rapped on the table, and said sharply: "Thank you, Mrs O'Rourke. Well, we do seem to have two very different ideas on how this festival should be run and what it should contain. I propose we vote with a show of hands, to choose Miss Bright and her young team's original plan, or the alternative way to go, proposed by Mrs O'Rourke. All those in favour of the first . . ."

"Excuse me!" Mrs O'Rourke interrupted loudly. "With all due respect, Guard Delaney, I think it would be fairer if we held a secret ballot."

There was a chorus of murmurs from the audience, some in favour, some against, and people began arguing. Barry Farrell stepped forward. He turned towards Emma Delaney and said: "Could I say a word, Madam Chair?"

Emma blinked at being addressed so oddly. Dessy said under his breath to Brendan: "Certainly, Mr Table!" Brendan grinned.

Emma said: "If you wish, Mr Farrell. After all, I was about to introduce you when we were interrupted." She glowered across at Mrs O'Rourke, and then rapped on the table for silence and said: "This, ladies and gentlemen, is Mr Barry Farrell, recently returned home from the USA, where he has had considerable experience promoting shows and other events. Mr Farrell."

Barry Farrell thanked her and the audience, and then gave a smooth and convincing speech about himself and his activities in the States, explaining that he would be happy to help to promote the Ballygandon Festival, perhaps even persuading Americans to come over for it, and that he would also be pleased to help with raising funds.

He ended by saying: "If I may say so, Madam Chair, I will be pleased to abide by the result of whatever voting method you choose, but since the idea of a secret ballot has been raised, I feel such a ballot might avoid any disputes in the future about who favoured which festival. As an impartial observer, I shall be happy to assist you in organising the ballot as speedily as possible."

Reluctantly, Emma Delaney agreed. She asked Molly to see if she could find some pads of paper in one of the cupboards behind the stage. Barry Farrell went across to talk to Joan Bright and Brendan and Dessy, who were looking fed up.

"I really think this is the fairest way to avoid any possible complaints," he said.

"I suppose you're right," said Joan Bright. "It just seems a lot of bother."

"I got the feeling most of the audience liked *our* plan," said Brendan.

"Well, we'll soon find out, won't we?" said Barry Farrell.

He went over to talk to Emma Delaney about the ballot. As he leaned over the table, Brendan saw him glance across to where Mrs O'Rourke was still standing beside her easel at the other side of the stage.

Brendan wondered if he could have imagined it, but he could almost swear that he saw Mrs O'Rourke gaze back at Barry Farrell, and give him a wink . . .

21

3

Baffling Ballots

"Will these do, Emma?" asked Molly, bringing a batch of small notepads across to the table and putting them down. They were the kind of small square pads people keep beside the telephone to jot down notes.

"Those will do fine, thanks Molly," said Emma. "Now could you all help me to tear off enough pages for the voting? They gathered round the table, Joan and the Ballygandon Gang on one side of Emma, and Barry Farrell on the other, and began tearing off pages.

"What shall we put them in?" asked Brendan.

"There were some cardboard boxes in the cupboard," said Molly, "with pencils and sellotape and stuff in them."

"They'll do," said Emma.

There were six boxes, and Emma put a batch of voting papers in each. Joan Bright and the Ballygandon Gang, with Mrs O'Rourke and Barry Farrell, went down the rows of seats giving out the papers.

"Quiet please!" cried Emma when they were all given out.

"Now, I want you all to write just one number on your paper. If you want to vote for the first plan which Miss Bright outlined, put the number One. If you want to vote for Mrs O'Rourke's plan, put the number Two. Fold your papers over, and then we'll go round again with the boxes and collect them."

There was a din of chatter in the hall. Some people put their heads together, discussing which way to vote. Others hunched their shoulders and held the voting paper cupped in their hands so that no one near them would see how they voted. There was much borrowing of pens and pencils.

While this was going on, Molly, Brendan and Dessy, together with Joan Bright, Mrs O'Rourke and Barry Farrell, came back to the front of the hall with their boxes and stood in front of the stage, waiting to go round and collect the completed papers.

Mrs O'Rourke smiled across at Joan Bright and said: "Your notions for the festival were worthy, Miss Bright – but not quite *bright* enough, I think you'll find." She gave a sneering chuckle.

"We'll see, won't we, when the votes are counted?" said Joan Bright, coldly.

"Yes indeed," said Mrs O'Rourke, "and may the best woman win!" They saw her look towards the audience, where Seamus Gallagher was sitting. He smiled and gave the thumbs-up sign.

"That pair *can't* be let run the festival. It would be a disaster!" said Molly.

"Do you think she and Seamus really know Raven well enough to ask him for a concert?"

"Seamus only knows low-life people," said Molly.

"Well, there have been some scandals in the papers now and then, about the sort of people Raven is mixed up with," said Brendan.

"Yes," said Dessy, "Ravin' Raven, they call him. Hey, how about this for a riddle? What was the name of the town where Shakespeare had all his wild parties?"

"Don't know, Dessy," said Brendan.

"Stratford-on-Ravin'!" said Dessy gleefully.

Just then, Emma Delaney stood up and rapped the table. The chatter subsided. "Thank you," she said. "Now if you've all filled in your ballot-papers, I'll ask our people here to collect them."

The boxes were passed along the rows and the audience dropped their folded papers into them. Then the boxes were brought on to the stage. Emma asked two people she knew in the audience up to help, and they and Emma sat behind the table.

"I'd be happy to help if I may," said Barry Farrell, "as an impartial observer."

"Thank you," said Emma. One by one the boxes were tipped out on to the table, and the votes put into two piles, the Ones on the right and the Twos on the left.

As they watched the counting, Brendan said softly: "I'm not sure I trust that fella Barry. There's something fishy about him."

Dessy said: "Remember the rhyme:

> *You'll have something fishy,*
> *In a little dishy,*
> *When the Vote comes in!"*

"I hope you're wrong, Dessy," Molly said.

Emma was writing on a pad in front of her. She looked to her right and left at the other counters, and said: "Are we all agreed?"

The others nodded. Emma stood up and rapped on the table for silence.

"I'm worried," said Molly. "Emma doesn't look pleased at all."

Then Emma spoke. "I can now announce the result of the voting. Those in favour of Plan Number One: 109 votes." There was a murmur from the audience. Brendan looked at Molly and held up his hands, with the fingers crossed. Emma went on: "Those in favour of Plan Number Two: 124 votes. So the ballot is won by Plan Number Two."

Mrs O'Rourke smiled and clasped her hands above her head in victory. Seamus Gallagher clapped loudly, so did a few other people.

"I can't believe it!" said Brendan angrily.

"Neither can a lot of the audience by the sound of it," said Dessy.

Indeed at that moment they heard the bellowing voice of Mr McGlacken the butcher, sounding out from the hall: "Objection! I demand a re-count!" Other voices took up the cry.

Emma Delaney rapped the table loudly. "Quiet please!" She shouted. "QUIET! I can assure you all that the votes were counted and checked." She looked around at her fellow-counters, and they all nodded.

But Mr McGlacken was chanting: "Re-count! Re-count! Re-count!" and a number of people joined in.

Emma rapped loudly on the table again and again, till finally there was silence. "Very well," she said, "if it will re-assure those who doubt the result, we will count the votes again."

"A waste of time!" spluttered Seamus Gallagher.

"Ridiculous," said Mrs O'Rourke.

Emma glared at her. "I said we will count the votes again! And this time I will allow up to six of the objectors, and six who are in favour of the result, to come on to the platform and watch the counting."

There was jostling and pushing as people tried to get to the platform. In the end twelve people were on the stage, including Locky and Mr McGlacken. They crowded round the table, and the counting began again.

"There's still some hope for us," said Brendan.

"I hope you're right," said Joan Bright. "It's such a shame, after all your plans and ideas. And so many people I talked to seemed all in favour."

They heard Emma say to the crowd peering down at the table: "Well, there it is."

Mrs McEntee, the large fussy woman who ran the newsagent's and sweetshop in the main street, stepped forward, pointing at the table. "I didn't see my vote there!" she exclaimed.

"How could you tell?" asked Emma.

"I write with this special purple pen," said Mrs McEntee, "and my Number One vote wasn't there."

"Re-count!" barked Mr McGlacken.

Emma said impatiently: "I'm sure your vote was in there somewhere, Mrs McEntee, but in any case one vote wouldn't affect the result. Now if you'd please go back to your seats . . ." Reluctantly, the twelve shuffled back down the steps, Mrs McEntee shaking her head and muttering, and Mr McGlacken growling to himself.

When the audience had settled down again, Emma said: "I have to tell you that, with the observers watching, the re-count has given us exactly the same result. 124 votes to 109 in favour of Plan Number Two."

Mrs O'Rourke stepped forward and shouted above the chatter of the audience and the clatter of chairs being pushed back: "Thank you all for your support, and now we can look forward to a rip-roaring razzamatazz of a festival here in Ballygandon!"

* * *

Next day, the Ballygandon Gang were on their way to the library. Locky was with them.

"You know something," said Brendan. "I think that vote was rigged. Mrs O'Rourke fixed it somehow, and I've a feeling that Barry Farrell had something to do with it."

"But how?" asked Molly. "Everyone was watching the votes being counted."

"I don't know," said Brendan, "but there was certainly something fishy about it."

Dessy began to chant: *"You'll have something fishy . . ."* but the others shut him up.

"This is serious, Dessy," said Brendan.

"It certainly is," said Locky. "If your suspicions are right, then the voting was a fraud.

But how could you ever prove it?"

"It looks like a job for the Ballygandon Private Eyes!" said Molly.

* * *

Joan Bright was clearly very disappointed, but she tried to console them. "You put so much thought and energy into the whole project, it seems such a shame it should be wasted. Why don't we put up the whole scheme again for *next* year's anniversary of the Ballygandon Revolution?"

"Next year?" cried Molly, Brendan and Dessy all together.

Locky smiled. "You see, Joan," he said, "the young have no patience. But I agree, it seems a shame not to do anything after all this planning. I know – Mrs O'Rourke's brash scheme doesn't include a pageant. Why don't we organise that, anyway?"

"Good thinking!" said Dessy.

"Great idea, Grandpa," said Brendan.

"I don't suppose Mrs O'Rourke will be too pleased," said Joan Bright.

"Mrs O'Rourke," said Locky "can go and . . ." He paused, clearly deciding to moderate his language in front of his grandchildren. ". . . and jump in the river!" he said finally.

"If we have the pageant," said Molly, "you'll get your chance to act the Earl, Grandpa."

"It's a deal," said Locky.

They all looked at Joan Bright. She smiled and said: "Well, I can't see how anyone can object to a pageant, it will just add to the fun."

"Great!" said Dessy.

"Mind you," said Locky, "I'm not sure I would describe the screeching and wailing of that Raven person as 'fun'. Still, everyone to his taste."

"He's certainly not to mine," said Joan Bright.

"I don't know. I kind of like some of his music," said Brendan.

"Maybe," said Molly. "It's all that strutting about and making faces and shrieking 'I'm the greatest!' that bugs me. Not to mention that headdress and those silly big black wings he wears."

"Do you think he'll really come?" asked Dessy.

"I doubt it," said Brendan. "It's probably some fantasy of Mrs O'Rourke's."

"She couldn't afford to pay his kind of money. That's for sure," said Molly.

"That reminds me," said Joan Bright. "Even if we're only going to put on the pageant, it will still mean getting some funds from somewhere, for the costumes and so on."

"And Barry Farrell won't give us anything now," said Brendan. "He said he'd back whoever won the vote."

"So who can we ask?" Dessy wondered. They all looked at Locky.

He shook his head. "Sorry, folks," he said, "my gee-gees still haven't found the winning- post."

"Hey, I've got an idea!" cried Molly. "Why don't we ask Billy Bantam? He's got lots of money from the movies, and he's always been very generous."

"*And* he's a member of the Ballygandon Gang – American branch!" said Dessy.

29

"It's worth a try," said Joan Bright. "Why don't you e-mail him now?"

* * *

In the computer room they found Internet again sleeping on the keyboard.

"That's the most computer-literate cat I ever saw," said Locky.

Molly picked up Internet and held her, stroking her head. The cat began to purr loudly.

Brendan typed the e-mail and sent it. "We won't get a reply till much later," he said. "It's the middle of the night in California."

"Let's go and plan out the route of the pageant," said Molly.

* * *

They walked to the edge of the town and then along the road for nearly a kilometre. They stopped at a gate that led into a big grassy field.

"I'm sure Joe Gorman would let us assemble here in his field," said Molly. "Then when we're all ready, we can march out on to the road, into town and then down to the park."

They sat side by side on the gate, imagining the scene as the brightly costumed procession would make its way into Ballygandon with music playing and banners waving and the crowds cheering.

Then Brendan said: "Look at that!" He pointed down the

road. They could see the sun gleaming on a shiny black sports car with the hood down, which was coming towards them. It screeched to a halt just beside them. They saw that the front of the car was shaped and painted to look like a giant beak.

In the car sat a young man in dark glasses, with a black feathered headdress. As they gazed, he stood up and looked towards them.

"Hi there, kids!" he said. "Can you tell me. Is this the way to Ballygandon?"

It was Raven, the rock star.

4

Raven the Rocker

"That's where I live," said Molly. "It's just down the road."

"Thanks," said Raven. "You want a lift?"

"Sure!" said Brendan.

"Wow!" said Dessy, as he and Brendan climbed into the back seat and Molly into the front beside the singer. "I'm Dessy," he said, "and this is my friend Brendan, and that's his cousin Molly. We're the Ballygandon Gang."

"Good to meet you, gang," said Raven. "OK, let's go!" He let in the clutch and the car roared away down the road. It went careering down the main street, as people on the footpaths turned to stare. The three in the car waved wildly, and Dessy tried to stand up to give a salute, but the car lurched forward and he sat back down again heavily.

Then Molly realised they had sped straight past her parents' shop and their house, and were heading up the hill and out of the town again.

"Ballygandon, here we come!" yelled Raven.

"We've come and gone again!" shouted Molly. "You've just driven straight through it."

Raven brought the car to a sudden halt. "So that was Ballygandon, that was!" he laughed. He stepped out of the car and looked back the way they had come. The others got out too. They all looked back down the hill.

They could see the whole town below them, and Molly began pointing out the landmarks: the pub, the church steeple, the library . . . then she said: "And that's our house and our shop at the far side of town from here. You can just see the chimney sticking up."

"A great little spot altogether," said Raven – without much enthusiasm, Brendan thought. He decided Ballygandon needed more of a build-up.

"And over there, on the top of the hill," he said, "is the famous O'Brien castle."

Raven gazed at the ruins, standing out against the sky. "What's it famous for?" he asked.

"Ghouls and ghosts and goggle-eyed zombies," said Dessy.

"Groovy," said Raven.

"We've had some weird adventures up there," said Molly. "There was a princess murdered there long ago, and her spirit makes strange things happen."

"I must pay her a visit some time," said Raven. "After all, I can see a whole bunch of ravens flying around in the ruins. They'll make me welcome, don't you think?"

Brendan knew the birds were crows, not ravens, but he just said: "I'm sure they will."

"But right now," said Raven, "there's someone I'm

33

supposed to meet. A guy called Seamus Gallagher. Do you know him?"

"Yes, we know him," said Molly grimly.

Raven noticed her manner, but he just said brightly: "Well, that's more than I do. He's kind of a distant cousin, but I met his daughter Dervla out in LA. She was quite a goer."

"And she certainly went!" said Dessy. He was about to say more, but Brendan and Molly shook their heads at him. They didn't want to tell Raven that Dervla and her father had been involved in a criminal scam where they had altered the headstones in a graveyard to fool rich Americans that their families were buried there. The Ballygandon Gang had exposed them, and Dervla and her father had spent a spell in jail. When the time was right, they could reveal what they knew, but in the meantime they wanted to find out what Seamus's little scheme was this time.

"Where are you meeting Seamus?" Brendan asked.

"On the phone he said something about an old barn he's going to convert into a scene for a disco, and for me to sing in too."

"That'll be Mrs O'Rourke's barn," said Molly. "We'll take you there."

"Great," said Raven. "Hop back into the car."

"Have you ever played in a barn before?" Dessy wondered, as they clambered in.

"Never," said Raven, "but there's a first time for everything, I guess. I told Seamus I'd do a few numbers as a favour, since he's organising the festival for charity."

He started the car and began to turn it round. Molly

looked over the back of her seat, and made a face at the pair in the back, raising her eyebrows and mouthing the word "Charity!". Brendan and Dessy grinned. They all knew the only "charity" Seamus ever supported was one that would fill his own pockets with money.

They directed Raven down the hill and then along a side road that led between straggly hedges down towards the river. Then they turned up a bumpy lane. "There it is," said Molly, pointing to a big, ramshackle wooden building in a field.

They got out of the car and looked over a gate at the building. There was moss growing on the roof, and some of the tiles were missing. The few window openings were boarded up.

"Well," said Raven, "it's not the most glamorous venue I've ever played in, I'll say that for sure."

"I don't know why they want to hold the disco here," said Molly. "It will need a lot of doing up."

"Well, it belongs to Mrs O'Rourke," said Brendan, "and she's a great mate of Seamus's. Maybe she'll charge the festival for using it."

"Let's take a look at it, anyway," said Raven. They pushed the gate open and went into the field. The doors of the barn hung off big hinges caked with rust. Brendan pushed at one of them but it was stuck.

"I'll lift it a bit from the bottom," said Dessy. "Then maybe you can swing it open." He knelt down and put his fingers in the gap between the door and the earth. "Up!" he said, heaving.

Brendan pushed the door and it swung in half a metre or so, and stuck again. Dessy only just got his fingers out in time, and fell back on to the ground. He got up and they peered in through the gap. It was dark inside, with a few thin shafts of light coming in through gaps in the walls.

"Let's hope the audiences find it a bit easier to get in!" said Raven, easing himself through the gap. The others followed. They looked around them in the gloom. All they could make out was a big empty space with an earth floor, and some sacks and boxes stacked here and there against the walls.

"There's not much to see," said Dessy. He put his hand to his mouth and called: "Yoo-hoo! Is anybody there? Come out, wherever you are!"

"Don't be an eejit, Dessy," said Brendan."There's no one here."

"There might be a rat or two," said Dessy. "Hey, Molly, why don't you do your Pied Piper act and play your tin whistle? That will bring them out."

Molly grinned, took out her tin whistle, and played a tune.

"You know why that tune brought all the rats out to follow the Pied Piper?" asked Dessy.

"No idea," said Raven.

"It's called Shake, *RATtle and Roll!*" said Dessy.

"So, we've got a comic here," said Raven, "and a great tin whistle player too! Maybe you could play with me at the festival?"

"I don't think I could," said Molly. She was flattered, but she remembered that Raven had been invited by Seamus and the rival festival group. Maybe they could get Raven on their side instead?

"Think about it," said Raven. "Now let's take a look

around this amazing concert hall! I've got some matches here, maybe that will give us a bit of light. Grab hold of these."

He gave a box of matches to Brendan, who lit one and held it up. They walked towards a pile of boxes against one of the walls. The match burned down to Brendan's fingers, and he shouted: "Ouch!" and dropped the match and stamped on it.

"Careful," said Raven, "we don't want to burn the place down before the show, do we? Let's sit on these boxes and wait for friend Seamus to turn up. He'll have to do a bit of explaining about how he's going to stage any kind of performance in here."

They sat down on the boxes. "Can I ask you something?" said Molly.

"Sure, ask away," said Raven.

"Why do you call yourself Raven?"

"Well, my real name is Horace Bronnigan, and I didn't think that sounded much like a rock star. And when I was at school I read this poem about a raven. It was very spooky. It was all about this crazy poet guy who had lost his lover, and was moping away in his room one stormy night. Then in comes this raven and perches above the door, and whatever he asks it, all it says is *Nevermore!* And so it's telling him he'll never see his lover again, even in heaven, and what's more he's never going to get rid of that gloomy old raven either."

"Cheerful stuff, eh?" said Dessy.

"Right," said Raven. "About as cheerful as a bunch of zombies with hiccups. So I thought I'd write this song called *Nevermore*, about lost love and all that sad stuff."

"I remember it," said Molly, and she began to play the

tune on her tin whistle: a haunting, melancholy air which filled the darkness of the barn and echoed around it.

"Hey, you're really good," said Raven. "We'll definitely do a gig together at the concert. OK?"

Molly looked at Brendan and Dessy. Brendan whispered: "You have to agree. That way we'll have Raven on our side, and we can find out what Seamus is up to."

"Right on," muttered Dessy.

"What are you lot whispering about?" asked Raven.

"Nothing," said Molly, "but if you really mean it, I'd love to play in the concert."

"Great," said Raven. "Now, let's take another look around this fantastic venue. Light the way, Brendan!"

Brendan lit another match, and they moved in a small procession towards the far side of the barn. Suddenly there was a clatter and a crash, and a figure stumbled in through the gap in the doorway, cursing. They heard a voice shout: "What's this? Who's there?" It was Seamus Gallagher. They heard him fumbling about, and then the beam of a torch shone at them.

"Hey, who are you?" he called. "Put out that match! This place is a firetrap!"

Brendan threw down the match and stamped on it. "Hullo, Seamus," he said.

They could see the bald head and the shambling figure of Seamus Gallagher behind the torch as he approached them. He stopped near them, and shone the torch beam first at one face and then at another.

"What are you lot doing in here?" he growled. "This is private property! Get out at once!"

"They're with me, Mr Gallagher," said Raven. "They were showing me around your marvellous concert venue."

Seamus shone the torch at Raven. He looked in amazement at the feathered headdress and said: "Oh! Right! Then you're the rock star, yes?"

"Yes, I'm Raven, and you asked me to meet you at this concert venue of yours."

"Exactly!" said Seamus. "Thanks for coming. I don't know how you fell in with these desperate gurriers, but anyway, you're here now . . ."

"They were very helpful," said Raven.

"That's as may be," said Seamus, "but right now, kids, I want you out of here. Mr Raven and I have plans to talk about."

Raven shrugged his shoulders, and said: "See you around, kids. And thanks!"

"See you," said Dessy. They went across the barn and out of the door, with Molly playing a snatch of *Nevermore* on her tin whistle as they went. They heard Raven laugh and say: "Good girl yourself!"

When they were outside the barn, Molly stopped playing. They stood near the doorway, listening to what Raven and Seamus were saying. They had moved towards the door and stopped there.

"How's Dervla?" asked Raven.

"Fine," said Seamus. "She's back in California. She was here for a while, but she didn't really care for it."

No wonder, thought Molly, since she was in jail. She grinned at the others.

"It was because I knew her that I came here when you

asked me," said Raven. "She was quite a girl, a real credit to you."

"Thanks," said Seamus, sounding surprised.

"Now tell me what you want me to do," said Raven. "I'll go along with your plans, as it's all for charity. It *is* all for charity, isn't it?"

"Oh yes, yes, yes!" cried Seamus. "Not a penny goes to anything else."

Again, the listeners outside smiled wryly at each other.

"Fire away then," said Raven.

"Well, I'm arranging a press conference here tomorrow afternoon," said Seamus, "and thanks to your name we should get lots of media coverage for the festival."

"A press conference *here*?" said Raven in a stunned voice.

"Well, not exactly *here*," said Seamus. "We'll hold it in the community hall."

"But this barn is the venue for the concert and the disco, am I right?"

"Yes and no," said Seamus. "What I mean to say is, we plan to have it here, but there may be certain developments which will enable us to have a more . . . comfortable arena."

"Whatever you say," said Raven. "You'll certainly have a lot to do to make this into a suitable place."

"Quite, quite," said Seamus, "but we can sort that out nearer the time. Meanwhile, you can be at the press conference tomorrow? 2.30 pm?"

"Sure."

"Where are you staying, Mr Raven? You are very welcome to a room at my pub in Killbreen. You'll find it most luxurious . . ."

Outside, Brendan and the others had to stifle their laughter. Seamus's pub was about the most scruffy and *un*-luxurious place in the whole county. They were relieved for Raven's sake when they heard him say: "Thanks, but I'm already installed at the hotel in the town."

"Well," said Seamus, "how about lunch at my pub, one o'clock tomorrow? I can ask my colleague Mrs O'Rourke, and we can brief you on the festival programme." "OK," said Raven. Outside, the listeners realised he and Seamus were about to come out. They scurried round the corner of the barn, away from the gate. They watched as the pair went out of the gate. They saw Seamus admire Raven's car, then shake hands with the rock star and move across to his own battered Landrover which was parked just along the lane.

As Raven's car sped away and the Landrover trundled after it up the lane towards the main road, the three of them came out into the field.

"We must be at that press conference tomorrow," said Molly.

"We'll be there," said Brendan, "and I'll make sure my father is, too!"

"What do you mean?" asked Dessy.

"He's a journalist," said Brendan. "It could be a good story for the papers. Especially as we can give him our own briefing about the festival. Then he'll be able to ask some really awkward questions!"

5

Festival Fisticuffs

Next morning, Molly, Brendan and Dessy were helping Molly's father stack the shelves in the shop, when Mrs O'Rourke came in. Molly's father went to the counter to serve her. He asked if her lodger was still staying with her.

"Yes indeed," said Mrs O'Rourke. "That's why I'm buying all these potatoes, for Irish stew. He just loves Irish stew. They can't make it properly in America, where he's been living."

Behind the stacks, Brendan and Molly looked at one another. Brendan whispered: "America? Do you think her lodger might be . . . ?"

"Barry Farrell!" said Molly. "Just what I was thinking too. And if he's staying with *her*, that means his offer to put money into the festival was bound to be for her plan and not for ours."

"He said he was an impartial observer," said Brendan. "That's why we let him help with the voting."

"Help with it, yes," said Molly, "and maybe he helped to fix the result too!"

"Hey, you lot," Molly's father called. "stop skulking over there, and give me a hand to get Mrs O'Rourke's groceries." The three of them came out from behind the stack.

"Well, there's a coincidence," said Mrs O'Rourke, staring at them. "I was just about to tell you something about these three, Mr Donovan. Now they can hear it themselves."

"Tell me what, Mrs O'Rourke?" asked Molly's father.

"You know that barn of mine, down towards the river?" said Mrs O'Rourke. Mr Donovan nodded. "Well, I'm sorry to say that your daughter and these boys were seen in there, with lighted matches. Very dangerous. You should really keep them under control."

Molly's father was annoyed. "They're perfectly 'under control' as you call it, Mrs O'Rourke, and I'm sure they wouldn't do anything dangerous."

"Oh, *are* you?" said Mrs O'Rourke sharply. "Well, perhaps you'd better ask them what they were up to, lighting matches in my barn."

"It's not true, Molly, is it?" her father asked.

"Well . . ." Molly hesitated.

"*I* had the matches, Mr Donovan," said Brendan. "But it wasn't dangerous. We were just using them to see. There's no light in there."

"So you don't deny you were lighting matches in my barn?" asked Mrs O'Rourke.

"No, but it wasn't like that . . ."

43

Molly's father was frowning at them. "I'll see it doesn't happen again, Mrs O'Rourke," he said. "Now, is there anything else you want?"

* * *

"I'm sorry, I'm afraid your dad wasn't too pleased," said Brendan, as they sat on the gate of the field outside Ballygandon, where they had met Raven. This time they were waiting for Brendan's father to arrive for the press conference. Brendan had persuaded him on the phone that there could be a newspaper story in the festival and the appearance of Raven.

"I'm not much of a fan of those rock stars or their music," Brendan's father had said, "but if it will help you with your festival plans, I'll come along."

"I think my dad was annoyed mainly because he had to apologise to Mrs O'Rourke," said Molly. "He can't stand her."

"That makes four of us," said Dessy.

They saw a battered blue car approaching from the direction of the town.

"That's Locky's car!" said Brendan, waving. The car stopped. His grandfather got out and said: "Hullo there, gang! What's this I hear you've been up to, setting fire to barns?"

"We *weren't*, Grandpa!" said Molly angrily.

"Only joking," said Locky. "I wouldn't believe anything that Mrs O'Rourke accused you of. I stopped by the store and your father told me you'd had a set-to with her. Do you want a lift? I was on my way to listen in at this press conference affair."

"We're waiting for my dad," said Brendan. "He's coming to cover the press conference."

"Good, I'll wait with you," said Locky.

* * *

"This is quite a reception committee!" said Brendan's father, pulling up beside the group and getting out. He greeted them all and then said: "Well, fill me in a bit more about the background to all this festival business."

They told him of all that had happened, and their suspicions that the voting had been somehow fixed so that their own plans were defeated. They told him about Raven too, and the dilapidated barn where there was supposed to be a disco and a rock concert.

"Seamus Gallagher was very shifty when Raven asked him about it," said Brendan. "He said there might be 'developments' which would mean the disco would be somewhere else."

"Anything that fellow does is likely to have something shifty about it," said Brendan's father. "We'll see what we can do to find out."

* * *

When they reached the community hall, Seamus was already there in the doorway, greeting people. They could see quite a few people seated inside, some of them local reporters and one from the radio station. There were a lot of Ballygandon people too, who had come out of curiosity, mainly to see Raven or simply to see if there would be any rows and arguments.

Seamus saw the Ballygandon Gang approaching, with Locky and Brendan's father.

"Sorry," he said, "these children aren't allowed in. Adults only."

"Don't be ridiculous," said Locky, "two of them are my grandchildren, and they've as much right to be here as anyone."

"Besides," said Brendan's father with a grin, "Brendan here is my photographer. Isn't that right?" He pointed at the camera Brendan had slung round his neck.

"Right!" said Dessy. "And we're his assistants."

"OK then," said Seamus reluctantly. "But any trouble, and you're out, do you hear?"

* * *

"He seems a bit nervous to me," said Brendan's father as they settled themselves in their seats. "I wouldn't be at all surprised if there's something fishy going on."

They looked towards the platform. Mrs O'Rourke was sitting there, behind the table, and Barry Farrell was beside her. They had their heads together, chatting.

"Discussing recipes for Irish stew, no doubt," said Molly.

"Where is this Raven fellow?" asked Brendan's father.

"I can't see any sign of him," said Brendan.

"Perhaps he's flapped his wings and taken off," said

Dessy. "Who could blame him for wanting to get away from that bunch?"

The audience was beginning to get restless. Brendan looked at his watch. "It's nearly a quarter to three," he said. "What are they waiting for?"

"Raven, perhaps," said Molly.

Dessy started a muttered chorus, chanting:

"Why are we waiting?
Why are we waiting . . .?"

Some people laughed and began to join in. Mrs O'Rourke frowned and looked over at Seamus by the door. She pointed at her watch. Just then they saw Seamus leaning out of the doorway, talking to someone outside. Then he looked back into the hall, and gave the thumbs-up sign to Mrs O'Rourke. He disappeared again.

Mrs O'Rourke stood up, and rapped on the wooden table for silence. Gradually the babble of chatter and singing subsided.

"Thank you all for coming," said Mrs O'Rourke. "We know you will be delighted to hear the plans of our committee for the forthcoming Ballygandon Festival, one of the greatest cultural events of the year."

"Where's Raven?" one of the press photographers called out.

"All in good time," said Mrs O'Rourke. "As I said, we will first of all be giving you an outline of the splendid programme of events we have planned . . ."

"Get on with it, then," said Locky.

Mrs O'Rourke glared at him. "Let me begin," she said, "by introducing my fellow committee members. This is Mr

47

Barry Farrell, who comes originally from this part of the world, but who has spent the last few years in the United States." Barry Farrell stood up and bowed. "Mr Farrell has kindly agreed to use his skills to help us with the promotion and the fundraising for our festival. Thank you, Barry."

She began to clap her hands. Some of the audience joined in lazily.

Barry Farrell said: "It is my great pleasure to be associated with this wonderful series of events which, as Mrs O'Rourke said, will be a festival that will become, I am sure, one of the cultural highlights of the year. It is, I think you will agree, a most interesting mixture . . ."

"In fact, a real Irish stew!" Dessy called out. Some people laughed, and Mrs O'Rourke frowned again.

Barry Farrell went on to list some of the events. As he spoke, the audience began to shift in their seats, and some of them started talking among themselves. Barry Farrell turned and looked anxiously backstage. Then Seamus Gallagher appeared from behind the curtains and whispered to him.

Barry Farrell said: "And now, without more delay, I will ask my colleague Seamus Gallagher to introduce the person whose presence I do believe will be the highlight of our festival."

Seamus stepped forward and said: "Ladies and gentlemen, I am proud to present to you the great, the one and only star of stage, screen and radio – none other than: RAVEN!!"

He pulled one of the curtains aside and on to the stage stepped Raven, in his feathered headdress, a black jumpsuit glittering with glass sequins, and on his back, two big black wings.

He came to the front of the stage and raised his arms so that the wings fanned out behind him. He really looked as if he were about to take flight. There were gasps and then loud applause from the audience.

Molly took out her tin whistle and played a few bars of *Nevermore*. Raven bowed towards her. Photographers, including Brendan, flashed their cameras. Someone called out: "Give us a song, Raven!"

"Sure!" The singer went to the side of the stage and picked up his guitar. He launched into a number called *Winging It*. Molly knew this one too, and played her tin whistle to accompany him. There were cheers and applause as the song finished. Raven bowed, and then held out his hand towards Molly, who stood up and took a bow too.

Mrs O'Rourke thanked Raven. Then she said: "Now I am sure you can all see why the Ballygandon Festival will be the success story of the year!"

Raven bowed and went backstage again.

They saw Mrs O'Rourke and Barry Farrell and Seamus put their heads together, congratulating each other. Then Mrs O'Rourke stepped forward and said: "Thank you all for coming, and we look forward to seeing you again at the festival in six weeks' time . . ."

Brendan's father stood up and said loudly: "Just a moment, please!"

"Yes, what is it?" asked Mrs O'Rourke impatiently.

"As a member of the press," said Brendan's father, "there

are one or two questions I would like to ask about the organisation of the festival."

"Very well," said Mrs O'Rourke. She glanced at Seamus, who was frowning.

"First of all, some doubt has been cast on the accuracy of the result of the voting for your festival plans . . ."

"What doubt?" said Mrs O'Rourke. "The vote was all honest and above-board."

"I can vouch for that," said Barry Farrell. "As an impartial observer, and promoter of the festival, I can assure you there is no doubt which plan succeeded. It was ours. I mean, of course, *theirs*."

"Just how impartial are you, Mr Farrell?" asked Brendan's father.

"Totally impartial! The best plan won."

"Let's vote again!" cried Locky.

"Don't be ridiculous!" said Mrs O'Rourke.

"I'd like to ask something else," said Brendan's father. "Am I right in thinking that you are planning to hold a disco and a concert in an old barn which you yourself own?"

"That's correct."

"And can I ask what facilities are available in this 'concert venue', whether it is licensed by the authorities for shows of this kind, and whether it has been inspected by the fire service to make sure it is safe?"

"All those things will be taken care of," said Mrs O'Rourke. "Now if that is the end of the questions, I declare this meeting closed."

"Answer! Answer!" shouted Locky.

"Shut up, you stupid old fool!" cried Seamus.

"Step down here and say that!" said Locky, pushing his way to the front of the hall and standing below the stage. "You're a crook, Seamus Gallagher. Everyone knows it."

The audience was standing, watching this dispute with interest. Seamus Gallagher was going red in the face. He rushed forward, tripped and plunged off the stage, shrieking. Brendan and Dessy caught him and broke his fall, and they all ended up in a heap on the floor of the hall, with Seamus cursing and growling, and Locky standing over them, shaking his fist. There were several flashes as photographers snatched shots they were sure would make great pictures with captions like *FESTIVAL FISTICUFFS!* or *BRAWL AT BALLYGANDON!*

Seamus scrambled up and retreated, fuming with anger. He was helped away by Barry Farrell, while Brendan's father took Locky's arm and persuaded him to move off.

The Ballygandon Gang came with them and made their way out of the hall. "Well," said Brendan's father, "whatever happens now, you've certainly helped to put the Ballygandon Festival on the map!"

"Up the Ballygandon Revolution!" called Molly, as they marched away, their fists raised.

6

Melodies and Mysteries

Next morning, Molly, Brendan and Dessy were throwing a ball for Molly's dog Tina in the yard outside the grocery shop. Tina was bringing the ball back to them each time and dropping it at their feet. It was getting more and more gooey from being in her mouth.

"This is yucky, Tina!" said Dessy, picking the ball up with one finger of each hand. "You'll have to clean up your act if you're going to be in the pageant."

"*Is* she going to be in the pageant?" asked Brendan.

"Of course," said Molly. "I'm going to put an eighteenth century bonnet on her, and lead her as a dog of the revolution."

"Maybe we could get Internet the cat into the show as well," Brendan suggested.

"She's too lazy to march," said Dessy.

Just then a dusty white van drew up outside the yard. A young man in a tee-shirt and jeans got out and went round to the back of the van and opened the doors. It was Sean, who always delivered the papers and magazines for the shop. He pulled a big bundle out of the van. Seeing the three in the yard, he called out: "Hi, kids! Got your papers here. Fling them in to your dad, will you, Molly?"

"OK, Sean," said Molly.

"Catch!" said Sean, throwing the bundle into the air. Molly jumped up and caught it high above her head.

"What a save!" cried Brendan, applauding.

"You'll make the World Cup team yet!" said Sean. "See ya!" He got back into the van and drove away at speed.

Molly was looking at the paper on the top of the pile. "Hey, this is the local paper," she said. "We *must* see that." She undid the string and took the top paper off the pile. "Have a look at that while I take the rest in to Dad," she said.

When she came back, Brendan and Dessy were standing with the paper open in front of them, grinning. Tina was standing looking at them hopefully and wagging her tail, with the ball on the ground in front of her. But they had more exciting things on their minds.

"Look at that!" said Brendan. "There's a picture of Raven with his wings spread out, *and* one of Locky with his fists up in the air!"

"Let me see," said Molly, peering over their shoulders. "Wow! And there's a piece by your father as well. *"FESTIVAL FROLICS,"* she read aloud. *"There were fists flying as well as Raven's wings, as a new festival was launched in Ballygandon yesterday . . ."*

"And look," said Brendan, "he goes on to say how a lot

53

of people don't like the plans, and there are doubts about the safety of some of the venues . . ."

"He's stirring it up all right," said Dessy.

An old blue car drew up in front of the yard. "Here's Locky!" said Brendan, as his grandfather got out. Brendan waved the paper at him. "You're a star, Grandpa!" he called. "Look at this!"

Locky was delighted with the picture. "What a pity I didn't get the chance to take on that Seamus!" he said. "I'd have flattened him with one punch."

"Of course you would, Grandpa," said Molly.

"And now's your chance!" said Dessy. "See who's coming down the road." They looked and saw a Landrover approaching. At the wheel was Seamus Gallagher. He stopped when he saw the group in the yard outside the grocer's shop. He got out and shouted across at them, taking care to keep behind the Landrover.

"Your father's got it coming to him!" he yelled at Brendan. "I'll have him in court for what he said about me and Mrs O'Rourke and the festival!"

"You and whose army?" said Locky, striding towards him.

"Take it easy, Grandpa," said Molly, catching hold of his arm. The idea of Locky and Seamus brawling outside her father's shop was alarming. Besides, she wasn't at all sure that Locky would get the better of the contest.

All of a sudden they heard a fierce growl from the back of Seamus's Landrover. They looked and saw the snarling face of his huge dog, Lonnigan. They heard Tina give a growl in return. Then without warning, Lonnigan leaped out of the Landrover and rushed up the yard towards Tina. Molly grabbed her dog by the collar and held her. "Get him away from her!" she shouted at Seamus.

"Lonnigan! Come here, boy!" Seamus called, but the dog took no notice. It launched itself at Tina with a bound, fangs gaping. Molly tried to shield Tina. Brendan and Dessy dived at the snarling dog and grabbed it. They wrestled with it as the dog barked and growled.

"The hose!" yelled Molly. "Grab the hose, Locky!"

Locky ran over to the corner of the yard where there was a hose attached to a tap in the wall. He turned on the tap and pointed the hose at the wrestling group. "Get out of it, Lonnigan!" he shouted. The jet of water drenched the dog and Brendan and Dessy too. They let go of Lonnigan who rushed towards Locky. But Locky pointed the jet straight at him. It had such force that it nearly knocked the dog over. Lonnigan yelped, then turned and ran out of the yard towards the Landrover. Locky pursued him with the hose, just as Seamus came round the front of the Landrover to try and get hold of the dog. The water jet splashed all over Seamus too, drenching him from head to foot. He gasped and gulped and cursed, as the dog jumped back into the Landrover, and stood on the seat, shaking himself.

"I'll get you, the lot of you!" Seamus shouted. Locky directed the hose at him again. Spluttering and swearing, Seamus scrambled back into the Landrover and drove away. Seeing her enemy leave, Tina gave a ferocious bark of triumph.

"Good girl, Tina," said Molly, stroking her. "You saw that horrible beast off, didn't you?"

"With a little help from her friends," said Brendan, as he and Dessy stood in the yard, dripping wet.

"Right!" said Molly. "Thanks, fellas! And thank *you*, Grandpa!"

"Any time," said Locky, going to turn off the tap. "You two lads had better go in and change."

Brendan and Dessy went into the house.

"Maybe we should have a water-hosing contest, as part of the festival," said Locky.

"You'd win for sure, Grandpa," Molly grinned.

"That's more than I seem to do on the horses these days," said Locky sadly. "Perhaps I should borrow your man Raven's wings for them."

"Well, now's your chance to ask him," said Molly in surprise, as she saw the sleek black sports car coming towards them down the road. She ran out and waved, and Raven came to a stop.

"Hi there!" he said, getting out. Then he saw Locky. "Hello," he said. "You're the guy in the paper, the one who wanted to sort out Seamus."

"That's me," said Locky.

"This is Locky, my grandfather," said Molly. "He was just saying he'd like to borrow your wings to help the horses he backs."

"A racing man, eh?" said Raven.

"Sure," said Locky, "for all the good it's doing me these days."

"You win a few and you lose a few," said Raven. "But you could do worse than put a few quid on my nag, Raven's Wing."

"I haven't heard of that one," said Locky.

"I'm with a syndicate that owns him," said Raven. "He's just starting this season. The trainer reckons he'll be a champion one day."

"Thanks for the tip," said Locky.

"Good to meet you," said Raven, "though I'd be glad if you didn't knock out my patron before the festival gets going."

"He deserves it," said Locky.

"What have you all got against him, exactly?" Raven asked. "I know he's a bit of a wheeler-dealer, but if he's willing to do something for charity, I'm happy with that."

"But that barn he's planning to stage the disco and the concert in, you wouldn't put a pig in it," said Molly.

"He says he's going to do it up really well for the day," said Raven, but Molly thought he sounded doubtful.

"Hey, I've just had a great idea!" said Molly. "I know exactly the right venue for your show!"

"Where's that?" asked Raven.

"The castle!" cried Molly. "The ruined castle on the hill! I know it sounds crazy, but . . ."

"It doesn't sound crazy at all," said Raven. "That's the one you pointed out to me, isn't it? The one with the ravens flying around? What could be better for a Raven concert?"

"We'll show you round it," said Molly. "Here are Brendan and Dessy now."

"OK, let's go," said Raven, "I was on my way back to Dublin, but I've got time to take a look around."

"They'll give you a great guided tour," said Locky. "I'll

see you around, Mister Raven. And I'll be looking out for Raven's Wing."

"Next week's her first outing," said Raven, "at Monksville."

"I was going there anyway," said Locky.

"I'll be there myself," said Raven. "Come and look me up in the owners' box. We'll have a few jars and cheer her on."

"Great," said Locky.

* * *

Raven drove them down the road that led towards the castle. They stopped at the bottom of the hill, and walked up the rocky path. Above them, the jagged ruined walls were silhouetted against the sky.

They made their way through a gap in the outer wall, and went into a large rectangular area with a big stone fireplace at one end. This had been the banqueting hall long ago. Now the floor was scattered with stones, and grass grew up between them. The wind sighed through the gaping empty windows. The crows cawed as they flew in and out.

Raven looked around, and put his hands on his hips. "Wow, this is quite a place!" he said. "What atmosphere. It's really eerie. No wonder they say it's haunted. What was the legend again?"

They sat down on a pile of stones. The Ballygandon Gang told Raven the tale of Princess Ethna, who had been murdered on the night before her wedding, here in the castle, all those centuries ago. Her family said the bridegroom's clan wanted to steal her treasure, and a feud started which lasted for many years of bloodshed and revenge.

Strange sounds and unexplained happenings had been experienced here in the castle and even in the library below, which had been the gate lodge and was connected to the castle by a secret passage. It was there in the library basement that a document was found which turned out to be Princess Ethna's diary.

"She was staying here in the castle, waiting for her wedding," said Molly. "She wrote about how happy she was, and described sitting at the window up in that tower and looking out on the lands that would be hers and her husband's soon."

"I remember she wrote something about hearing a voice on the wind," said Brendan.

"That's right," said Molly. "It went something like:

'I hear your voice in the wind,
I see your face in the sky,
I am so happy, and I know why.'

"That would make a great song," said Raven. "I'll write it for the festival. I'll call it *Princess Ethna's Song.* And I'll launch it right here. This will be a great venue for the concert. We'll get the lights up here, and the loudspeakers and all. It will be a rave."

He began to hum a few bars of music, then started singing a melody using the words that Molly had spoken. Molly took out her tin whistle and played the tune. Then she stopped suddenly and said: "Listen!"

There was silence. Then, mingled with the sighing of the wind, they seemed to hear a high, melancholy voice, taking up the melody. It floated above them, as if it belonged to the ruined walls and the arched windows that towered above them, a voice that had first been heard here, hundreds of years ago . . .

7

Fire!

They listened in silence for a while, then the voice seemed to blend in with the sighing wind and disappear.

"Yes," said Raven quietly, "this is a great venue, that's for sure. What atmosphere! Maybe I could use a shot of it on the cover of my next album. Raven among the ravens, eh?"

"I can take some pictures now if you like," said Brendan, holding up his camera.

"Why not?" said Raven. "Supposing I stand here on this stone, so I'm framed against the sky by that ruined arch?" He jumped on to the stone and struck a pose, with his arms out.

"A pity you haven't got your wings with you," said Molly.

"I *have* got them!" said Raven. "Great idea, Molly."

"Where are they?" asked Dessy, half wondering if the wings might suddenly sprout out of Raven's back.

"They're in the car," said the singer.

"I'll run down the hill and get them," said Dessy.

"Race you," said Brendan.

"You're on!"

The pair of them were already scrambling over the wall when Raven said: "You'd better take these." He produced some car keys and threw them over to Brendan, saying: "The wings are folded up in a black satchel in the boot, with the headdress."

Brendan and Dessy raced off down the rocky path.

Raven said: "Got your tin whistle, Molly? Let's do a bit more work on the new song."

* * *

As Brendan and Dessy arrived back, puffing and out of breath, they heard the music of the tin whistle, and the voice of Raven humming the tune and making up words as he went along.

Molly stopped playing and asked: "Well, who won?"

At the same time, Brendan and Dessy both said: "I did!"

Raven laughed, and took the satchel Brendan handed over to him. He took out the wings and unfolded them, then put his arms in the harness that held them to his back. Then he put on the black feather headdress.

"You look like a real raven," said Dessy. "Hey, what did the raven say about the pelican?"

"Don't know, Dessy," said Brendan with a sigh.

"He said, 'He looks fierce, lads, but don't worry – his *beak* is worse than his bite!' "

"The jokes get worse by the day, Dessy," said Brendan.

"Thanks," Dessy grinned.

Raven climbed up on to the rock in front of the ruined arch. He stood there, and spread his wings out, his head up and his chin jutting out. "How's this?" he asked.

"Great," said Brendan. He knelt down, pointed the camera upwards at Raven, and took a picture. Raven struck another pose, and Brendan clicked the camera again. Raven moved to different parts of the castle, with Brendan following him, snapping all the time.

"He's enjoying this, I reckon," said Dessy.

"Stars like to be in the spotlight," said Molly.

"Yes, we do!" said Dessy. He jumped up on a big rock and flung his arms in the air like Raven had, but then he lost his balance and fell off.

"I shouldn't leave the nest just yet, if I were you, Dessy," said Molly, laughing.

Raven came across to them, saying: "It's time I was getting back to Dublin, folks. Thanks for showing me round Princess Ethna's castle. I'll be down in a few weeks for the festival. Send me the pictures will you, Brendan?" He took a card from his pocket and gave it to Brendan.

"Sure thing," said Brendan. He looked at the card, which was black with white printing on it, giving Raven's name and address. Brendan saw that it just said RAVEN, not his real name, HORACE BRONNIGAN.

"Can I give you a lift back?" Raven asked.

Brendan said: "I'd like to stay and take a few more shots of the castle. It will be sunset soon, and it should look good and spooky."

"Spooky is right," said Raven, packing away his wings and headdress. "See you then!"

"You should really say *'Well, I must fly!'*" said Dessy.

"I'll leave the gags to you, Dessy," said Raven. He gave a wave and set off down the hill.

* * *

Brendan took more pictures, while Molly played her tin whistle and Dessy practised some of his yo-yo tricks. The sun was setting. Brendan stood at one of the ruined windows, looking out over Ballygandon. "The town looks really good in this light," he said. He pointed the camera and took a shot. "Maybe we could use a picture for the festival programme."

"What programme?" said Molly sourly. "Don't forget it's still Mrs O'Rourke and Seamus's lot who are organising the festival."

Brendan was looking through his camera lens. "Funny you should mention them," he said. "I think I see the pair of them, right now. I'll just put on my telescopic lens."

"Where are they?" Molly asked.

"Outside the old barn, talking," said Brendan.

"They're probably deciding how to do it up into a disco venue," said Dessy sarcastically.

"And how to charge a fortune for getting in," said Molly. "They'll get a shock when they know Raven has decided to play here instead."

"They've gone into the barn," said Brendan.

"Let's go," said Molly. "It's getting cold up here."

"Flap your wings," said Dessy. "That'll warm you up."

"I'll flap your head in a minute," said Molly, grinning.

* * *

They made their way down the path. Brendan stopped to take another picture in the fading light. Molly looked across the town. "That will make a cosy picture," she said, "with the smoke curling up from the chimneys, and all."

Brendan stared through his lens. "That's not a chimney," he said suddenly. "It's coming from the roof of the barn!"

"Yes, I can see it now," said Molly.

"And there are flames too," said Dessy.

"Seamus and Mrs O'Rourke are inside," said Brendan. "We'd better get down there!" They ran down the path and then along the lane that led past the field where the barn was. They could see the roof really blazing now, and hear cracking and splintering as beams crashed down.

They went into the field and towards the door of the barn, but clouds of smoke came billowing out as they approached. They began to choke. They could see flames inside the barn now.

"We'll never get in there," said Molly. Then they heard the sound of the fire engine, coming down the road towards them. In front of it was Seamus's Landrover. It stopped by the gate and Seamus got out to open it so that the fire engine could get into the field.

"At least he got out of the barn in time," said Molly, "but where's Mrs O'Rourke?"

As Seamus opened the gate, they saw him look across and recognise them. He shouted up at the driver of the fire engine: "Look, there they are! Caught red-handed! I'll get them!" As the fire engine roared into the field and the firemen started spraying hoses on to the blazing barn, Seamus came rushing towards them.

"Run for it!" cried Brendan, and the three of them ran past the barn towards the far side of the field. They saw Seamus stumble and fall, then pick himself up. They were able to scramble over the fence and into the lane. Coming up the lane they saw a white garda car, followed by Mrs O'Rourke's van. They both stopped at the gate into the field. Emma Delaney got out of the garda car and Mrs O'Rourke out of her van. They saw Seamus rush over to them and point down the lane. They crouched down, then crept through a gap in the hedge into the field on the other side of the lane. It was where Mrs O'Rourke kept the horse-drawn caravans she hired out to holidaymakers. Through the hedge they could see Emma Delaney get back into the garda car, and Seamus and Mrs O'Rourke into her van. The car and van came towards them down the lane.

"Quick! In here!" said Brendan, pointing to one of the caravans. The three of them scrambled into the caravan and crouched down behind the door. They heard the car and van go on down the lane. Before long they came back and stopped in the lane nearby. Emma got out and went over to the van.

They heard Mrs O'Rourke say: "They must have got away across the fields towards the river."

"Are you sure it was Molly and her friends?" asked Emma.

"Absolutely!" said Seamus.

"*And* we'd seen them before, playing around with matches in the barn," said Mrs O'Rourke. "I tried to tell Molly's father about it, but he wouldn't listen."

"Well, I'll go and have a word with her parents," said Emma Delaney. "I'll tell them what you said, and I'll talk to the kids too. First we've got to make sure the fire is under control."

As they moved on up the lane, Brendan peered cautiously out through the window of the caravan. "They're still hosing," he said, "but the flames seem to have died down. Now there's mostly a lot of smoke."

"We can't risk running for it yet," said Molly. "We'll have to wait till the fire's out and they've all gone."

"But if we go back to your house then, they'll come and arrest us," said Dessy. "They think we started the fire."

"We can tell them we saw Seamus and Mrs O'Rourke going into the barn," said Brendan.

"But who'd believe she'd set fire to her own barn?" asked Dessy. "It doesn't make sense."

"And she'd already complained to Dad about us and the matches," said Molly.

"There's nothing else for it," said Brendan. "Until we can prove we didn't do it, we'll have to go on the run."

"Where to?" asked Dessy.

"I don't know," said Brendan. "We'll find somewhere to hide out."

"What about the old boathouse down on the river?" Molly suggested.

"Perfect," said Brendan. "We'll wait till the coast is clear, and go across the field."

"I'm hungry," said Dessy. He pulled a bag of sweets out of his pocket, and offered them round. They were mainly toffees which had softened in his pocket and stuck together.

"Well, it's better than nothing," said Brendan, as he pulled one toffee away from another. "Thanks, Dessy."

They chewed and waited. Finally they heard the voices of Emma Delaney and the firemen, saying everything was OK now. The fire engine moved off, and so did Emma's garda car.

Brendan looked out into the gathering dusk.

"Seamus and Mrs O'Rourke are standing talking by the gate, and looking over at the barn," he reported. "Now they're walking down the lane. They're coming this way."

They could hear Seamus saying: "Where could those horrible kids have got to? I saw them come this way."

"Never mind," said Mrs O'Rourke. "They'll turn up some time, and then the guards will bag them. Lucky we saw them with the matches, eh? It will put the guards right off the scent."

Seamus laughed. "Juvenile delinquents!" he sneered. "They deserve all they get."

"And so do *we!*" said Mrs O'Rourke. "I'll have that insurance claim in, first thing in the morning. Lucky I upped the figure so much, wasn't it?"

"You're a smart woman, Mrs O," said Seamus, "and when we get that insurance money, we can hire a really fancy place for the disco and the concert, and with what we'll charge people to hear that Raven character, we'll be raking it in!"

As they moved away, Brendan said: "Well, now we know who started the fire!"

"But how can we prove it?" asked Dessy. "That pair will just deny everything."

"We'll think of a way," said Molly. "The coast is clear now. We can go down to the boathouse."

"I wish we had some food," said Dessy. "These sweets won't last long."

"I know what," said Molly. "There's a store shed at the back of our house, I'll go and get something from there. I can sneak round the back without being seen. And I'll stop at the phone box on the edge of town, and ring to say we're OK. Otherwise they'll be sending out search parties when we don't come home."

"Your parents might realise where you're ringing from," said Brendan.

"That's true," said Molly. "I'll phone Locky instead, and he can let them know."

* * *

When she got back to the boathouse, she was weighed down by a large sack she was carrying. "I got some cereals and cans of beans and soft drinks," she said, "and I found some old sacks as well, to do as blankets. I brought a torch too."

"Wonderful," said Brendan, as they began to unpack the things. "Did you manage to phone Locky?"

"I did," said Molly. "I'm afraid he wasn't too pleased. He said my parents would be worried, and we should really go home."

"You didn't tell him where we were hiding?"

"No, I just said we'd come back as soon as we could, and I'd ring him tomorrow. Finally he said he really didn't approve, but he'd call my parents and tell them we were safe."

"Thanks a lot, Molly," said Brendan, and they began to spread out the food and drink on an old wooden bench.

"This is great," said Dessy. "A dinner and a night in the Boathouse Hotel!"

"It's certainly better than a night in jail," said Brendan, "which is where Seamus would like to have put us."

"And where he ought to be himself," said Molly. "And you know who will make sure he goes there?"

They all chorused together: "The Ballygandon Private Eyes!"

8

On the Run

The boathouse was a rickety old wooden structure that had not been used for years. It had a ramp that went down into the water, so that boats could be launched into the river or hauled out. The only boat to be seen here now was a wrecked rowing boat with many of its planks broken. It lay half under water, at the bottom of the ramp.

"Brendan, you're a seafaring man," said Dessy, pointing at the wreck. "Maybe you'd like to sleep on the deck there?"

"Thanks, Dessy, but I'll stick to dry land for tonight. This bench will do me fine."

"There's only room for one on that," Dessy complained.

"Then I think Molly should have it, don't you?" said Brendan. "We can sleep on the wooden floor."

Dessy felt he had to agree, but he said: "Let's finish our dinner first, anyway."

They put the torch so that it shone along the bench at

71

their unusual meal. They opened the tins of beans and poured them out on slices of bread and munched them, washing them down with gulps from a can of lemonade. Then they shared a bar of chocolate.

"We'll keep the cereal for breakfast," said Molly. She gave them each one of the big sacks. They climbed into them like sleeping-bags. "Are you sure you don't mind me sleeping on the bench? We can take it in turns if you like."

"No, I'm so tired I could sleep anywhere," said Brendan, settling down on the floor. Dessy did the same.

"If you're both OK," said Molly from the bench, "I'll turn off the torch to save the battery."

When their eyes got used to the darkness, they could see thin shafts of moonlight coming through the gaps in the roof where tiles had come off. The river lapped gently at the side of the boathouse. Lucky it was a fine night, thought Molly as she gazed at the moonbeams. She felt her eyelids growing heavy.

"First thing tomorrow," she said, "we'll have a council of war. OK?"

There was no reply. The other two were already fast asleep.

* * *

When Molly woke, the sky was getting light and the birds were twittering in the trees beside the river. She climbed out of the sack, her joints feeling stiff. She stretched and waved her arms. Then she went out on to the river bank and knelt down and splashed her face, scooping up handfuls of water. That would have to do for a wash just now.

She heard Brendan's voice: "You're not drinking that, are you?"

"No, just having a splash-wash. Mind you, the water's probably not too bad to drink. The fish live in it, after all."

Brendan splashed his own face and said: "Maybe we could catch a fish for breakfast. I should have brought my fishing-rod."

"I don't fancy raw fish," said Molly.

"The Japanese eat them all the time," said Brendan.

"Rather them than me," said Molly. They washed out the baked-bean tins in the river, then put some cereal in them and poured on lemonade.

"Hey, that's not too bad," said Dessy, crunching away. "I might make beans and lemonade my regular breakfast. That reminds me, what did they call the man who went into the grocery store and shot all the cornflakes packets off the shelves?"

"Tell us, Dessy," said Molly.

"A Cereal Killer!" Dessy grinned.

Molly and Brendan smiled, and began packing the empty cans into the sacks. They didn't want to leave any evidence of where they had been. Then they sat down on the bench for the council of war.

"We've got to find some proof that Seamus and Mrs O'Rourke went into the barn just before it caught fire," said Brendan. "If only I'd thought of taking a long-distance picture when I saw them."

"You still couldn't prove when it was taken," said Molly.

"We'll have to go back and see what's happening at the barn," said Dessy.

"It's too risky," said Brendan. "If they saw us wandering about in the ruins of the barn the guards would nab us straight away. They think we did it, don't forget."

"And the fact we ran away will make them sure of it, I'm afraid," said Molly. "But I think Dessy's right. We've got to find out what's going on there."

"Let's go for it!" said Dessy.

* * *

After making sure there was no one around, they walked along the river bank to the bridge which would lead them back towards the fields. They stopped to bundle up the sack of rubbish and hide it in a hollow in the bank. After they crossed the bridge they went along the towpath and then through a gap in the hedge into the field. The six caravans Mrs O'Rourke hired out stood in the field. It was still very early, so even if there were holidaymakers in any of them, they were not up and about yet. The horses were in another field further along the river.

"Suppose she's hired the caravan we hid in, and there's someone there?" whispered Brendan as they crouched low and moved across the field.

"She can't have hired it out last evening," said Molly. "She was too busy setting fire to her own barn."

Indeed, they found the caravan just as they had left it, and climbed in. "So far so good," said Dessy.

Brendan peered out through the window. "There's no one around yet," he said. Molly found another window, and Dessy squinted round the edge of the doorway. Parts of the ruined barn's walls were still standing, jagged and charred, but the roof had gone, apart from a few blackened beams. A bird sat on one of them, chirping away.

After half and hour or so, they decided that one of them could keep watch, while the other two sat down on the cushioned benches round a small table at the back of the caravan.

"I wouldn't have minded having this bench to sleep on last night," said Dessy.

"If we're going to find any evidence," Molly said, "we'll have to sneak out and have a look around in the ruins. Maybe no one will come for a while yet."

"We'll have to put that plan on hold for a bit," said Brendan at the window. "There are people arriving."

They all looked out, and saw two cars coming down the road and turning into the lane beside the field. One was the garda car, the other a smart blue Mercedes. The cars stopped near the gate. Out got Emma Delaney, the guard, with Mrs O'Rourke. The driver of the other car stepped out with Seamus Gallagher. The driver was a tall man in a dark suit and black hat. He was carrying a large black briefcase. He had a small clipped moustache and a stern expression. He looked with a frown at the muddy ground, as Seamus swung the gate open and ushered him into the field. He must have been thinking he should have worn wellies instead of his smart polished city shoes.

However, he followed Mrs O'Rourke and Emma as they led the way across the field, with Seamus at the rear. They stopped beside the gap where the barn doors had been, and looked inside.

The smooth man opened his briefcase and took out a large notebook and a pen. He closed the briefcase and handed it to Seamus to hold. He made a few notes, then went into the barn. The others followed.

"That fella must be the man from the insurance company we heard Mrs O'Rourke talking about," said Molly.

Through the gaps in the broken-down walls, the three watchers could see them moving around inside the ruined barn, while Emma Delaney examined the walls and floor, and Seamus and Mrs O'Rourke pointed and gestured to show the insurance man how the barn used to be. Suddenly Emma bent down, picked something up and held it in the air. It was a metal canister.

"What's that?" asked Dessy.

"It looks like one of those big cans that hold paraffin," said Molly. "We sell them in the store, for lamps and stoves and such-like."

"Slosh some of that around, and you'd have no trouble getting a fire started," said Brendan.

"No trouble at all," said Molly.

They watched as the four people emerged from the barn and stood outside the door. Emma had put the paraffin can into a big transparent plastic bag. The insurance man was looking at it with great interest. He tipped it upside down. There was nothing in it. Emma Delaney was talking on her mobile phone.

"There's all the evidence we need!" said Brendan. "She's probably phoning the garda station now, so they can put that pair under arrest."

But they saw the four come back across the field to the

gate, without any sign of screeching squad cars arriving, or handcuffs being produced.

"They must have decided to go quietly," said Dessy uneasily.

They saw the group stop in the lane outside the gate. Seamus and Mrs O'Rourke were pointing down the lane. They saw the insurance man ask a question, and Seamus put his hand out, about four feet above the ground. Then he held up three fingers to illustrate what he was saying, and pointed down the lane again.

"I'm sure they're talking about *us*," said Molly. "They're showing the insurance bloke which way we went yesterday."

"But now they've found the can . . ." said Dessy.

"Don't you realise?" said Molly. "They're trying to pin the blame on us! They're probably claiming that we sloshed the paraffin around and set it alight. And the can probably came from my father's store, so they'd reckon we could easily have stolen it."

As they watched gloomily, the four got back into the cars, which moved back up the lane and away. Brendan bent to pick up his camera which he'd put down on the bench. Suddenly he said: "Hey, look at this!" He pointed under the bench.

They all gathered round to look. On the floor was a paraffin can, exactly like the one they had seen Emma Delaney holding up. Dessy bent down to pick it up, but Molly said: "Don't touch it! We don't want our fingerprints on it. It could be evidence. This must be where they stored the paraffin. It would be simple enough to come over and get a can to take into the field and into the barn without being noticed."

Brendan pushed the can with his foot. He couldn't move it. "This one must still be full," he said.

"We'll leave it just where it is," said Molly. "Then when the time is right, we can tell the guards where to find it."

"Why not now?" asked Dessy.

"It still might not be enough proof," said Molly. "Listen, they won't come back to the barn for a while, I'm sure. There's just time for us to get over there and poke around to see if there's anything else we can find."

* * *

They were able to creep out and across the lane, then through the hedge to the back of the barn. There was no one around. They climbed through a gap in the wall and knelt down so that they couldn't be seen. The barn was a wreck. It had looked dilapidated enough before, but now it was empty except for the charred remains of some of the boxes, and bits of blackened beams and tiles that had fallen from the roof.

They began to crawl around on the floor which was strewn with ashes. They started sifting among the tiles and bits of wood. Suddenly Molly cried: "Look at that!" She pointed at the floor. There lay a yellow torch, just like the one that Seamus had used when he found them in the barn with Raven.

9

Accusations

"That's Seamus's torch, I'm sure of it!" said Brendan, reaching down.

"Don't touch it!" said Molly. "If they find our fingerprints on it, they'll suspect us even more."

"If we leave it here," said Dessy, "Seamus may come and find it before the guards do."

"And if we take it away, there's no proof of where we found it," said Molly.

"I'll take some pictures of it," said Brendan, holding up his camera, "a close-up, and some distance shots to show where we found it in the barn." He began focussing his camera.

"Then we'll get out of here," Molly said, "and ring Emma Delaney, to tell her what we've found."

She and Dessy waited while Brendan took the pictures, glancing nervously at the door in case someone came. Then they heard a sound out in the field: a loud series of barks.

"They've set the police dogs on us!" said Dessy in alarm.

"No, they haven't," said Molly. "I know that bark. It's Tina!" Sure enough, at that moment her dog bounded in at the door of the barn, barking excitedly. She rushed over to Molly, delighted to have found her, and began nuzzling her, barking and wagging her tail wildly.

Molly knelt down and tried to quieten her: "Shush, Tina, shush! Good girl! Quiet now, quiet!"

Brendan put his camera in its case and said: "We'd better get out of here, quick!"

"I've got some chocolate left," said Dessy. "Perhaps that will keep her quiet." He took the remains of a chocolate bar out of his pocket and held it out to Tina, starting to unwrap it. But the dog seized it all and began to run round and round the barn, delighted with herself. "She thinks it's like the ball we throw for her," said Molly. "Here, Tina, here!"

But instead of coming to her, Tina stood where she was, and began chewing at the chocolate, wrapper and all. Molly crept towards her, saying: "Good girl, Tina!" Just as she reached the dog and tried to grab her, Tina swallowed the last of the chocolate and started to run round the barn again. The three of them ran after her, trying to catch her. Tina clearly thought this was another game, for she kept running and dodging.

Finally she ran out of the door of the barn and into the field.

They ran after her and another chase began. Tina dashed back into the barn again, and they were about to follow when Molly pointed at the lane beside the field and said: "That's done it! Look, it's my father's van!"

Coming towards them down the lane they saw the old van with DONOVAN GROCERS on the side. Molly's father was at the wheel, and he didn't look pleased. There was nothing they could do now, except wait for him. Mr Donovan stopped the van and angrily pushed open the gate into the field. "Molly, come here at once!" he shouted. "And you boys too!"

As they moved reluctantly towards the gate, he went on: "What do you think you're up to, running off like that? We've been worried sick about you."

As Molly approached her father, she said: "But, Dad, didn't Grandpa phone you?"

"He did, and he said you were safe, but that wasn't much help, was it? Your mam and I were sick, wondering where you were and what had happened to you. It was so stupid and thoughtless to run off like that."

"I'm sorry, Mr Donovan," said Brendan, "but . . ."

"I should hope you *are* sorry!" Molly's father snapped. "It was only thanks to Tina running away too, that I found you at all. Now get in the van right now, all of you! We're going straight back to tell your mam you're all right."

"But, Dad," said Molly, "we've got to ring the guards. We've got new evidence. . ."

"Never mind that, I'll be ringing Emma Delaney myself – she was as worried as we were. Now get in!" Brendan and Dessy climbed into the back of the van glumly, and Molly was just about to get in too, when she suddenly cried: "Tina! Where's Tina?" She looked around the field and called Tina's name again and again. There was no sign of her. Molly ran across to the barn and looked in at the door.

"There you are, Tina!" she cried, as she saw the dog trotting around the barn, snuffling at all the smells, and scratching at the tiles and bits of wood that were strewn around. Tina came over to her and this time Molly was able to grab her collar. "Good girl, good girl!" she said, bringing Tina over to the van. She and the dog scrambled in and Molly pulled the door shut.

* * *

Once Molly's mother had hugged her and thanked heaven she was safe and unharmed, she switched to being just as angry as Molly's father had been.

"I don't know which of you thought this little jaunt up," she said, "but you should all be well and truly punished for causing us all such trouble and worry. You must go and telephone your mother and father at once, Brendan, and tell them you're all right."

"Oh, did you tell them we were missing, Mrs Donovan?" Brendan groaned.

"Of course I did! We're supposed to be looking after you! Though your poor mother must think we're not doing a great job. I doubt if she'll let you stay here again."

"Really?" Brendan was shocked. He loved staying in Ballygandon. In many ways it was a lot more fun than being at home in Dublin.

"Yes really!" Molly's mother was saying. "Go and telephone at once! I'd have rung your parents too, Dessy, but I didn't know where they were."

"Neither do I, half the time," said Dessy cheerfully.

"Well, my father, anyway, he's on the road most of the time, and my mother's looking after the younger ones. She doesn't worry too much about where I am."

As Brendan went to telephone, he almost wished his parents were the same.

* * *

They had to use a lot of persuasion to ask Molly's father when he talked to Emma Delaney to tell her they had urgent evidence about the fire, and they could show it to her straight away. Emma was relieved they were all right, but like Molly's parents she was annoyed at all the worry and trouble they'd caused.

"If you hadn't turned up today, we'd have had to send out a search party," she said sternly, as they drove with her in the garda car towards the barn. "You know there's a serious offence called *Wasting Police Time*? Well, I just hope this visit we're making isn't going to be another example of it."

"No, we did really find the torch, and we're sure it belongs to Seamus," said Molly.

"Be careful. Don't bandy accusations about too freely, or you could be in trouble," said Emma. "I know Seamus has had criminal convictions, but there has to be proof. The paraffin can is being examined by the forensic people, but your father says he stocks them, so like Mrs O'Rourke claims, it *could* have come from his store, and you *could* have taken it."

"You don't believe that, do you Emma?" said Molly.

83

"No, I don't," Emma replied, "but you see what I mean about accusations and proof?"

"Sure, but this torch will *really* be proof," said Molly.

"We'll see," said Emma.

They had had quite a problem persuading her to come down to the barn and see what they had found, and quite a problem too persuading Molly's mother and father to let them go. They had said that the three of them would be 'grounded', and have to stay home for two days. They had pleaded about having to go to see Joan Bright and get their pageant plans going, but Molly's parents said that would have to wait.

"It could still be *our* festival," said Molly hopefully. "We've only got to prove how that ballot was rigged, and then we can take over."

"I know you're great detectives," said Emma Delaney, "but you'd be wise to concentrate on one crime at a time. Let's sort out this barn fire first."

* * *

Once more they walked the muddy path that led from the field gate to the barn. They went in through the doorway. Everything seemed to be as they had left it.

Molly walked across to the pile of burned tiles where they had found the torch. "This is where we found it," she said, pointing. Then she looked down in horror. The torch had gone!

* * *

"I'm sure they'll find the evidence," said Locky to Molly's mother and father, back at the house. "They wouldn't say they'd seen it if they hadn't."

"But they might have imagined it," said Molly's mother. "Those three are always playing at detectives and crooks."

"But let's face it, they *have* got results in the past," said Locky. "I'm sure they're showing Emma Delaney the evidence right now."

* * *

But in the barn, the situation was less hopeful.

"I can't see any torch." Emma looked at them with a frown.

"It . . . it was *there*, I'm sure of it!" said Molly.

"So am I," said Brendan.

"Me too," said Dessy.

"Well, where is it now?" asked Emma. "You know what I said about wasting police time?"

"It was there!" cried Brendan. "I've got photographs to prove it. I'll give you the film."

"It must be here somewhere," said Molly, almost tearfully, as she knelt down and began to scrabble among the blackened tiles and bits of wood. Then she sat back in despair.

"Seamus must have come in and taken it," said Dessy.

"But he didn't know we'd found it," said Brendan, "and it's only an hour or so since we were here ourselves, and Tina found *us!*"

"Tina!" Molly sighed. "That's the answer! Remember when Dad arrived and we were out there talking to him?

Tina went running back into the barn, and I had to come in here to find her. She was in here on her own for ten minutes or so. When I came in she was running around, sniffing and digging. She must have picked the torch up thinking it was another game like the chocolate bar, and run off with it and buried it somewhere."

Emma Delaney was impatient. "Games? Chocolate bars? What *is* all this rigmarole? I've had enough. I know you kids are trying to help, but you've led us on enough wild-goose chases for the moment."

"But if we just search a bit longer . . ." pleaded Brendan.

"No, that's it!" said Emma. "I'm bringing you back home, and I won't be sorry if your mother makes you stay there for a while, as she said she would. Come on." She walked out of the barn. The three members of the Ballygandon Gang looked at each other gloomily. Brendan shrugged his shoulders. There was nothing more they could do for now.

Or perhaps there *was*, he thought suddenly. He had remembered the can of paraffin they had found under the bench in the caravan.

"Just a minute," he said to Emma as he came out of the barn. "There's something else . . ."

He stopped short in surprise, as he saw Mrs O'Rourke striding across the field towards them.

"Good morning, guard," she said with a sneer. "I see you've rounded up the Usual Suspects, and brought them to the scene of the crime."

"Not exactly," said Emma Delaney. "Our inquiries are continuing."

"Well, I hope they won't take much longer," said Mrs O'Rourke. "It's obvious that these three ruffians are the culprits. The sooner they're charged, the sooner we can settle the insurance claim."

"Can I say something?" said Brendan.

"What is it this time?" Emma Delaney was beginning to get annoyed.

"We were hiding in that caravan in the field down there . . ." Brendan pointed down the lane.

"In my caravan?" Mrs O'Rourke snapped. "You were trespassing! I'll have you charged for that, too."

"Well, Brendan?" asked Emma.

"I know we shouldn't have been there," said Brendan, "but we weren't doing any harm, and under one of the benches we happened to see a paraffin can, just like the one you found in the barn."

"Really?" said Emma with some interest. She looked at Mrs O'Rourke, who had gone a bit pale. She glanced from Emma to the others. She licked her lips nervously.

Then with brazen confidence, she said: "Of course you found a paraffin can! I keep one in each of the caravans, so my clients can light their paraffin stoves for picnics. In fact I found only the other day that there was one missing from one of the caravans. *Now* I know who took it!" She glared at Molly, Brendan and Dessy.

"She's lying. We *didn't* take it!" cried Molly.

"No way!" said Brendan.

"Prove it," said Mrs O'Rourke.

"I've had enough of people flinging accusations about!" Emma Delaney sounded really angry. "From now on, I'd like you to leave it to us professionals to find out if this fire was accidental or not, and if it wasn't, who caused it. Please don't come near this barn again, Mrs O'Rourke, until we've completed our investigations. And that applies to all the rest of you too." She glared at the Ballygandon Gang. "Goodbye, Mrs O'Rourke, and as for you three, I'm taking you straight back home."

As they tramped off forlornly across the muddy field with Emma Delaney, Mrs O'Rourke smiled and said: "Goodbye! See you in court!"

10

Masks and Messages

Molly's mother and father wouldn't be persuaded to relax their ruling.

"No, we said you were 'grounded' for two days, and that's it," said Molly's mother.

"But there's the festival," Molly pleaded. "We've got all the preparations to make."

"Then you'd better start making them here," said her father.

"Please, Mr Donovan, can't we even go outside?" asked Brendan.

"All right. Into the yard if you like, but no further."

* * *

Out in the yard, Molly, Brendan and Dessy began kicking an old plastic football to each other. Tina joined in, snapping at the ball. Then the dog pushed it into a corner and began chewing at it, spluttering and growling happily at the same time.

"Tina, Tina, give us our ball back!" said Brendan, going across to her and reaching out his hand. But Tina snarled at him, then went on chewing. Soon there was a hiss of air from the ball.

"She's punctured it!" cried Dessy.

"Please, Tina, give it here!" said Molly, seizing the ball. The dog wagged her tail and held on, with her teeth gripping the tear she had made. Molly pulled, but Tina still held on. Molly backed across the yard and Tina followed, still gripping the ball. She was enjoying this new game, which looked like some odd kind of Tug-of-War.

"I'll give you a hand!" said Brendan, and he grasped Molly's waist to help pull her backwards. Suddenly there was a tearing sound and the ball came apart. Tina and Molly were each left holding half of it.

Dessy clapped his hands. "A great contest!" he said. "I declare the result, One All. One All, but No Ball!"

"You're right there, Dessy," Molly smiled, holding up the ragged half of the football.

"Hey, I've got an idea," said Brendan, taking it from Molly. He put the curved piece of plastic over his face. "Behold, the mask of Frankenstein!" he boomed.

"Stop trick-acting, Brendan," said Molly. "It's time we started to make our plans for the festival. It'll be something to do while we're grounded here."

"But that's the idea," said Brendan. "We can start by making these bits into two masks. They're just the right size. We'll cut some eyeholes, paint a face, and tie them on with string."

"Yes, for the pageant!" said Molly. "The townspeople were all in disguise for the Earl's visit. We can make a whole lot of masks like that."

"Yes, I bet the local team will be delighted to let us cut up all their footballs," said Dessy. "They could play the first half of the match with the first half of the ball, and the second with the second."

"You're a scream, Dessy," said Molly. "We'll get something else for the other masks. There's a whole stack of empty cardboard boxes in the store shed. We can cut them up. Come on, let's investigate."

* * *

The store shed was a large wooden building in the far corner of the yard. They found the boxes in a pile against one wall. They had held groceries for the shop.

"These will do fine," said Molly, picking one up. "I'll go and get some scissors and string. You two get some of those sacks from the pile over there. We can cut arm and neck holes in them to make costumes."

She came back into the shed with the scissors and string and a box of coloured markers to draw faces on the masks. They set to work.

* * *

"Well, folks, how do I look?" asked Dessy. He had his head and arms sticking through holes in a sack. A mask was tied on to his face. It was white with big black eyebrows and a black painted moustache, and it had streaks of red all over it that looked like blood.

"Who are you meant to be?" asked Brendan.

Dessy held his arms in the air and chanted:

> *"Beware Horace O'Toole,*
> *The Ballygandon Ghoul!"*

He advanced stiffly towards them. Then he put his hands around Brendan's neck.

"Get off, Dessy!" said Brendan, pushing him away. Then he held his own mask in front of his face. It was made from one half of the ball, and was painted like a clown's face, white with a red nose and red cheeks.

"Great," said Molly. "Now we've got a ghoul, a clown . . . and a *witch!*" She held up the other half of the ball, which she had painted green, with a grinning red mouth. They all tied their masks on, put on sacks, and began prancing around shrieking and groaning and cackling with laughter.

"Merciful heavens, it's Halloween night already!" cried a voice at the door. They all stopped and looked across the shed. There was Locky, peering in at the curious scene. They explained that they were getting ready for the pageant by making disguises.

"Don't forget, Grandpa. You're going to be the Earl of Dunslaggin in the procession," said Molly.

"Proper order," said Locky. "I always feel I was born to be noble. What shall I wear?" He looked doubtfully at the sacks draped on the Ballygandon Gang.

"I suppose a sack wouldn't do for an Earl," said Dessy.

"Hey, what do they call it when an Earl gets up at six o'clock in the morning?"

"Well, Dessy?" asked Locky.

Dessy grinned and said: "EARLy Rising!"

"Nice one, Dessy," said Locky, as the others groaned. "But look, I've thought of a costume I could wear. One of the ladies who lives at Horseshoe House has a posh red velvet dressinggown with a white fur collar. I'm sure she'd lend it to me for the show. It would look really aristocratic on me."

"Terrific, Grandpa," said Brendan.

"Dessy's going to be Horace O'Toole," said Molly.

"That's me," said Dessy proudly. "Horace O'Toole, the Ballygandon Ghoul."

"Ah yes, he's the one that gets thrown in the pond, isn't he?" said Locky.

"Just a minute," said Dessy, "I'd forgotten about that bit. Maybe I'm not quite right for the part after all. You need someone a bit. . . taller!"

"No, you're just right," said Molly, "though we might get you a slightly different costume. If only we could go to the library to plan it all with Miss Bright. She knows all about it."

"Oh, that reminds me," said Locky. "That's what I came to tell you. All this capering about made me forget. Joan Bright phoned from the library – she wanted to talk about the pageant with you too. Your mother asked me to tell you."

"And I suppose she said we were grounded for two days," said Molly.

"She did at first, but I did a bit of persuading for you. She says you can go to the library, but only for a couple of hours, and then you must come straight back."

"Nice one – thanks, Grandpa," said Molly.

"We Earls have our uses, you know," said Locky.

* * *

Locky walked with them to the library. On the way they saw a few posters in shop windows for the Ballygandon Festival. They were on bright day-glo yellow paper, with big black print, saying:

COME TO THE BALLYGANDON MONSTER BASH!

The posters listed the events Mrs O'Rourke had described at the meeting: a disco, the Miss Ballygandon Contest, a casino and a poker competition, and then the words:

STAR ATTRACTION!
RAVEN THE ROCKER!
IN PERSON!

Then it went on to say that advance booking was essential, and tickets could be bought from Mrs O'Rourke or from Gallagher's pub in Killbreen.

"They'll make a packet from that," said Molly. "I wonder if Raven knows what they're at."

"He must have told them about the change of venue," said Brendan.

"He said they told him it was all for charity," said Locky. "but since it's the last event, Mrs O'Rourke and Seamus may well slip away with the money before the concert even begins."

"We'll have to warn him to watch out," said Molly. "We'd better phone him."

"Better still, you can tell him in person if you like," said Locky. "I'm going to that race meeting at Monksville where his horse is running next week. I'll take you along."

"We'll be 'de-grounded' by then," said Dessy. "But Molly, will your parents let us go?"

"We'll have to ask Earl Locky to use his charm again," Molly grinned.

* * *

Joan Bright was pleased to see them at the library. She said she had had an e-mail from Billy Bantam saying that he'd arranged for some money to be available for her at the bank in the nearby town.

"Of course," she went on, "we can't use it now our festival isn't going on. We'll have to arrange to send it back."

"Let's not do that yet," said Molly. "There's still time for us to find out if the ballot was rigged, and get our festival on instead."

"Whatever happens, I think we've got Raven on our side," said Brendan. They told Joan Bright about their visit to the castle, and his decision to stage the concert there. "I'm sure Mrs O'Rourke was relieved," said Joan Bright.

"They certainly can't stage it in the barn, and from what Emma Delaney told me, she won't be getting the insurance money for a long while yet, if she ever does. Emma doesn't believe you had anything to do with it, though there's not enough evidence to charge Mrs O'Rourke and Seamus yet. But there's enough to make the insurance people suspicious, and to delay any pay-out."

"They'll still try to make money from the concert with their ticket sales," said Molly. "But we're going to warn Raven to make sure it goes to charity instead of to *them*."

"And we decided to do our pageant anyway, didn't we?" said Brendan.

"Yes, indeed," said Joan Bright. "That's what I wanted to plan with you all."

"My theatrical friends here have already begun on the costumes," said Locky. "They are sensational, believe me!"

They began to plan the pageant. Finally Locky looked at his watch and said: "It's nearly time I brought you lot back home, as I promised. We don't want your grounding to be extended so that you can't come to the races."

"Can we just send an e-mail reply to Billy first?" asked Brendan.

"OK, but get a move on," said Locky.

* * *

In the computer room, they had to lift Internet the cat off the keyboard where she was sleeping, before they could log on. They sent the e-mail thanking Billy for the money and saying how their festival had hit some snags, but they

96

hoped it could go ahead, once the ballot-rigging of their rivals could be proved.

When the screen told them their message had been sent and Brendan was about to log off, Internet jumped up and walked across the keyboard.

"Just as well she didn't do that while we were e-mailing Billy," said Molly. "I don't know what he'd have made of that message!" She pointed to the screen which said:

9999999999999999ggggg0000000######pppppppp

They laughed, and Brendan again reached to turn the machine off.

"Wait!" said Molly suddenly, staring at the screen.

It had begun to flash on and off, and underneath the gobbledygook made by Internet's paws, some more letters were appearing:

KMLJ HL BSOSYFM EMO NLBR

"Where did they come from?" asked Dessy, wide-eyed. "The cat's over there on the chair; she can't have done it – unless she's got some strange powers over the machine!"

"*She* hasn't, but someone else may have!" said Molly excitedly.

"You mean . . ." Brendan began excitedly.

"Princess Ethna!" said Molly, as they gazed at the screen, feeling a sudden chill come over them all.

11

Raven at the Races

"It's some kind of code," said Brendan. "and it happened before, don't you remember? When they found Ethna's old diary down in the library basement, and Miss Carr stole it, and the message helped us to track it down?"

"It's weird," said Dessy, "but then so are all these internet messages flying around in cyberspace."

"Look at the screen!" said Molly urgently. "It's flashing on and off – and the message is getting fainter."

"I must write it down!" cried Brendan. "Then we can crack the code later." He grabbed a piece of paper from the desk and began scribbling the letters as Molly called them out: "KMLJ, then a gap, then HL . . ." The letters were getting fainter. Just as she finished, they faded out altogether. At that moment, Internet decided to join in, and jumped up on to the keyboard.

More jumbled gobbledygook letters came on to the screen:
Xxxx88888#####bbbbbb//////////nnnnn

"Thanks, Internet!" Molly laughed. "That was great timing!"

"Yes, we'd have had a problem decoding that," said Brendan.

"Not at all," said Dessy, "I can read it. It says *Miaow Miaow Miaow!*"

* * *

They decided not to tell Joan Bright and Locky about the message and where they thought it might have come from.

When they got back into the main library, Locky was looking at his watch anxiously. "We'll have to be getting back home," he said. "Time's running out."

"I must go and pick up that book that fell out of the shelves just now," said Joan Bright. "Internet sometimes prowls around and knocks the books down."

Molly and Brendan looked at one another. They knew Internet had not been in the library.

"I'll do it," Molly said.

"Thanks, it's just over there," said Joan Bright, "in the Local History section."

Molly went across and picked up the book. It was a book of ghost stories. Molly knew it well. It was the one that contained the account of Princess Ethna's murder, and the haunted castle at Ballygandon.

* * *

When they got home, Brendan started to try and work out what the coded message said. He looked up a book about codes, but none of them seemed to be right. He just couldn't find the key. Molly persuaded him to take a break and help them get ready for the pageant. She found some half-finished cans of paint and some brushes. They tore up more cardboard boxes and painted squares of cardboard to look like flags.

"Flags are supposed to flap in the wind,"said Brendan, as he sploshed blue paint on the cardboard.

"Not always," said Dessy. "Remember those flags the astronauts planted when they got to the moon? They were completely stiff."

"That's because there's no wind on the moon," said Brendan.

"Ah, the moon expert!" Dessy grinned. "You'll be telling us next that it's made of green cheese."

Brendan flicked his brush at Dessy, and a splodge of blue appeared on his forehead. Dessy flicked his brush in return, scoring a red bullseye on Brendan's nose. They flicked some more, trying to dodge out of the way at the same time.

"Stop it, you eejits!" cried Molly eventually. "You'll have us grounded for even longer."

Brendan and Dessy stopped. They looked at each other and laughed. Molly joined in. "I know what you can be in the pageant," she said. "Neapolitan ice creams!"

* * *

When they were free to go out again, they decided to go up to the castle. Maybe they would somehow get another clue to the code up there.

As they walked along the street, Dessy said: "We should have brought some of those cans of paint. We could have sploshed it all over those festival posters."

"We could always tear them down," said Brendan, going across to one of the shop windows.

"Not such a good idea," said Molly. "The people would think we were just vandals, and not fit to hold a festival of our own."

When they got to the castle, they tried to imagine what it would be like when Raven staged his concert here.

Dessy climbed on to a big rock and flapped his arms like wings. He whistled some bars of music, but Molly said, wincing: "Dessy, you haven't got a tune in your head. Listen." She got her tin whistle out and began to play the melody they had been singing with Raven. As she played, they all seemed to hear, very faintly, somewhere in the air among the towering ruins, a faint, high voice, joining in . . .

* * *

Locky was able to persuade Molly's mother and father to let him take them to the races at Monksville. For an hour, they rattled along the country roads in Locky's ancient car. It was a fine day with a blue sky scattered with a few fluffy clouds.

Dessy pointed at two birds sitting on a fence as they passed. "Look!" he said. "Ravens! That must be a good sign."

"They're magpies," said Brendan.

"But they're still lucky," said Molly. "Remember the old rhyme about seeing magpies,

One for sorrow,
Two for joy?"

"That *has* to be a good omen," said Locky. "It will be a joy to *me* for sure, when Raven's Wing beats the whole field!"

* * *

When they got to the racecourse, they had to park in a field and walk down the road to the entrance. The road was crowded with people. There were families with children, coming for a day out, groups of young men in jeans, laughing and larking about, jaunty characters in natty suits and tweed hats with feathers in them, with folded racing papers tucked under their arms. Locky had his own racing paper sticking out of the pocket of his coat. Before they set off they had seen him at home sitting at the kitchen table, circling the runners he fancied. They noticed there were two big circles around Raven's Wing in the fourth race.

They went through the arched entrance to the race-course, where Locky paid for their admission tickets. The stands and the racetrack were still some distance away. On either side of the path as they walked they saw booths selling burgers and sandwiches and ice creams. There was a tent too, and through the entrance they could see a play area for children, and fairground stalls where you could get a prize for shooting at toy ducks, or throwing rings over a coloured stick, or darts at a dartboard.

"I'm good at darts," said Dessy. "I think I'll have a go at that."

"Later," said Locky. "Right now we must go and find Mr Raven in his special box."

Brendan was puzzled. What kind of box did Locky mean? He imagined a horse-box, the kind they used for taking horses to and fro on the roads, behind cars. Surely that wouldn't be grand enough for a racehorse owner?

They passed the parade ring, where the horses and jockeys for the first race were walking round in a circle. People in smart jackets or anoraks were standing about, and stable boys and girls led the horses along confidently. The punters crowded at the rails, making notes on their racecards, and pointing or nodding as the horses passed them.

Then they came to the enclosure where the grandstands were. At the entrance, Locky produced a large blue card with the words OWNER'S GUEST printed on it in gold letters. The man at the entrance pointed to the stand in the middle, then looked with a frown at Locky's three companions.

"It's all right," said Locky. "They're with me. We're all guests of Mr Raven."

The man looked up a list on a clipboard, ran his finger down it, then said: "OK. In you go."

They made their way through the crowds in the open enclosure in front of the stands, till they came to a gate that said: CORPORATE HOSPITALITY.

Locky showed his blue card to another man, and they went up some stairs that led through open terraces with seats to a door at the top. After going through a bar and a restaurant, they finally found Raven on a private balcony with chairs and a table with glasses and bottles on it. "Hi there!" said Raven. "So you found the place all right. Would you like a drink? There's champagne here, Locky, and whatever the Gang would like too. It will soon be time for the first race."

The balcony had a marvellous view of the racetrack. They could look down on the finishing line and the winning post. On the other side of the rail they could see a huge video screen. Just now it showed the scene further away, where the jockeys were getting their horses up to the starting gates.

"They're off!" said a commentator's voice from the loudspeakers, and they watched as the horses bounded out of the gates and began thundering down the track.

* * *

They joined in the cheers and shouting as the horses approached the finish, bunched close together, the jockeys' shirts a jumble of colours as they urged the horses on. It was a close finish, with a horse called Festive Frolic winning by a short head.

"Did you have anything on that, Locky?" asked Raven.

"No, I'm saving it all for Raven's Wing."

"Good thinking," said Raven. "I'm sure you can't go wrong there."

Locky thought back on all the times he had heard those words from people giving him tips for horses they claimed were certain to win races. More often than not, they were wrong.

There was still more than an hour to go before the fourth race when Locky would find out if this tip was wrong or right. Brendan asked if they could go down and have a look around.

"Sure," said Locky, "but mind you're back in time for the big win!"

* * *

Down on the ground, they walked past the line of bookies' stands where the odds for the horses in the next race were being shouted out, and scrawled on the board behind each stand. Punters were eagerly handing over their cash.

"It's a pity we haven't got any money to put a bet on," said Dessy.

"Maybe it's just as well," said Brendan. "Look how often Grandpa loses!"

They wandered back past the parade ring and towards the main entrance. They went into the big tent and Dessy tried his skill at darts. He won a prize and gave a cry of delight. He was expecting money, but all he got was a little plaster statue of a woman with no arms.

"That's a bit gruesome, isn't it?" he said as they walked out of the tent. "They might have finished it off."

"It's a model of a really famous statue, you eejit," said Molly. "Look, it says on it there: *The Venus de Milo*. The arms had broken off when they dug it up."

Dessy looked at the statuette and asked: "What did the sculptor say when they told him his statue of Venus looked angry?"

"What, Dessy?" Brendan wondered.

"He said 'It's all right, she's totally *'armless!'*"

Brendan raised a mock fist at Dessy, who ran out of the tent. Brendan and Molly chased him. He ran round the back and came to a stop at a slatted wooden fence that had been put up at right angles to the tent.

"OK," said Dessy, "I give up."

Just then they heard voices on the other side of the fence.

"OK folks, give it another try. All you've got to do is *Find the Lady!*"

"He can have this lady if he likes," said Dessy, holding up the statuette. They peered through the gaps in the slats of the fence. They could see a man in a baseball cap standing behind a trestle table. He had three playing cards face up in front of him. There were two Aces and one Queen. There was a group of about thirty people clustered around the table.

"Who'll bet me twenty quid they can *Find the Lady?*" said the man in the cap, holding up the Queen card.

"You're on!" said a man in the crowd, coming forward. He had curly black hair, and was holding out a twenty-pound note which he put on the table.

"Here we go then," said the man in the cap. He put the cards face down in a line, then picked them up and quickly shuffled them from side to side and over each other several times. Then he left the cards face down in a row and stood back.

"Well, which is she?" he asked.

The curly-headed man stepped forward and put his

finger on the middle card. The other man turned the card face up and said: "You win!" It was the Queen. He pulled a twenty-pound note from his pocket and handed it over. "You're too sharp for me, sir. That's the second time you've won. At this rate I'll soon be broke. OK, once again, folks! Who'll have a go this time?"

A fat man in a crumpled suit stepped forward and put his twenty-pound note on the table.

The man in the cap shuffled the cards around again, and the man pointed to the card on the left. When it was turned up, it was one of the Aces.

"Bad luck, sir!" said the man with the cards. The fat man grunted angrily and walked off.

Other people tried and failed to pick the Queen. Then the curly-haired man tried again, and won.

Molly said: "I think that guy with the curly hair looks very familiar."

"Me too," said Brendan. "Hey! Just a minute. I think that hair is a wig. Imagine if he was bald, and look at the face."

"Wow, that's it!" said Molly. "It's Seamus Gallagher!"

Just then they saw Seamus look at the card-shuffling man and point urgently. Quickly the man in the cap gathered up his cards and stuffed them in his pocket, saying: "That's all for now, folks!" He and Seamus hurried away, and mingled with the crowds. As they went, the card-shuffler took off his cap and stuffed it in his pocket.

Brendan gasped. "We know *him* too!" he said. "It's Barry Farrell!"

Two guards arrived and began questioning people. Some of them pointed the way Seamus and Barry had gone. The guards hurried off after them, but there wasn't much chance they could catch up with them now.

* * *

On the way back to the grandstands, they stopped for a hamburger at one of the kiosks. As they munched, Molly asked: "What do you think they were at?"

Dessy said: "I know. It's a scam my brother has told me about." Dessy's brother was into all kinds of activities on the wrong side of the law. "It's called the Three-Card-Trick," Dessy went on. People try to keep their eye on the Queen card when he turns it face down. But the guy with the cards shuffles them around so cleverly, that the card they're certain is the Queen, always turns out to be the Ace."

"But Seamus got it right," said Brendan.

"Of course he did," said Dessy. "There's a mark on the back of the Queen no one else would notice. Seamus was pretending to be an ordinary punter to make the others think it was easy to find the Queen. It's a confidence trick, and that pair are con artists. That's why the guards were after them."

"*Now* I realise how they did it!" said Brendan.

"How who did what?" asked Molly.

"How they rigged the ballot. Remember Barry Farrell was one of the people counting the votes. If he can shuffle cards like that to fool people, why couldn't he have shuffled the ballots, and put some of his own fake Number Two papers in place of real Number Ones?"

"You've got it, Brendan!" said Molly. "But how can we prove it?"

"Only by finding the real ballot papers he managed to take away," said Brendan. "And I have a hunch that that coded message might tell us where they are."

"Wouldn't he have just got rid of them afterwards?" asked Dessy.

"He might have thought it was too risky to keep them with him. It's my guess he hid them somewhere in the community hall."

"We'll go and hunt for them as soon as we get back," said Molly.

Just then they heard the loudspeakers announce that the fourth race would begin in ten minutes.

"Come on," said Brendan. "We've got to go and watch Raven's Wing come up with a big win for Grandpa!"

12

The Great Procession

As they passed the bookies' stands, they saw that the odds on Raven's Wing were mostly at ten or eleven to one, which meant that Locky could make quite a packet if the horse won. This was the big race of the day, so there was a feeling of excitement among the crowds as they made their way up to Raven's balcony.

There they found Locky and some of Raven's friends in the music business. Raven was scanning the racetrack with big binoculars. The giant video screen showed the horses gathering behind the starting gates. Raven pointed out his horse, a sleek, jet-black animal whose jockey was also in black, with a white zigzag design like a lightning streak across his silk shirt.

There were ten other horses in the race, all ambling around, and Raven's Wing was tossing his head and being patted and calmed down by the jockey.

"I guess he's nervous, it being his first race and all," said Molly.

"Almost as nervous as I am," laughed Raven. Suddenly he leaned down and picked up his black feather headdress and put it on. He gave a war-whoop which made some of the nearby spectators turn round, startled.

The cry of "They're off!" came from the commentator. The horses leaped forward and were soon galloping in a packed bunch close to the rail. As the race went on, they began to string out, with a grey horse with a jockey in red and white stripes, nearly a length in front.

They heard the commentator say: "And it's the favourite, Bagshot's Folly already taking the lead, with Job Share second closely followed by first-time runner Raven's Wing . . ."

"Raven's Wing! Raven's Wing! Come on Raven's Wing!" Brendan, Molly and Dessy were shouting together. They could hear the shouts swell up around them among the huge crowd in the stands, many of them urging on Bagshot's Folly. Raven was giving war-whoops and punching the air with his fists.

Now they could see the horses in the distance, galloping down the straight towards the finishing post below them; and there they were in close-up too, on the video screen. The roars and shouts were deafening now, as the commentator nearly exploded with excitement, his words tumbling out: "It's neck and neck as they come to the finish, with Bagshot's Folly leading by a nose, and with two hundred yards to go, it looks like the favourite's race . . . but no, coming up fast on the inside is Raven's Wing . . ."

111

Everyone in the box was shouting and waving, and Brendan, Molly and Dessy were jumping up and down, as they watched the black horse slip by the favourite and pass the winning post with its head just nudging in front of Bagshot's Folly as they crossed the line.

"Raven's Wing it is," cried the commentator, "winning by a nose from Bagshot's Folly, with Babbling Betty a length away in third place . . . and what a sensational race for this first-timer, a dark horse in every sense of the word . . .!"

On the balcony, they were all hugging one another and shouting for joy. Raven took off his headdress and waved it around and Locky threw his hat high in the air. They watched it spin away in the breeze and disappear in the sea of heads way down in the stands below. Locky didn't care. He gave Raven a great slap on the back and shouted: "Raven's Wing forever!"

* * *

Locky was singing as they rattled along in his ancient car on their way back to Ballygandon. He made up a version of *Old Macdonald had a Farm,* which went:

> *"Old Man Raven had a Wing,*
> *Ee-eye-ee-eye-o!*
> *And on that wing he had a horse,*
> *Ee-eye-ee-eye-o! . . ."*

They all sang along happily.

On the way back to the car they had told Locky about Barry Farrell and Seamus Gallagher and the three-card trick they had seen.

"Those fellas would be up to anything to make money," said Locky. "Why can't they just make it by backing the horses, like the rest of us?" He grinned and patted his chest where a great deal of cash nestled in the inside pocket of his jacket. He said he'd buy the whole family a slap-up meal in the big town to celebrate, *and* he'd be able to help them now with some funds for the festival.

"Our festival won't get the go-ahead unless we can find those hidden ballot papers," said Brendan.

"As soon as we get back, we'll go and search the community hall," said Molly.

* * *

"The balloting was done here, at the table," said Molly, as they stood on the stage. "Maybe he stuck them to the underneath of the table." She bent down and looked, then said: "No luck."

"I'm still sure the answer's in here somewhere," said Brendan, spreading his notebook on the table and studying the coded message. "I've tried all kinds of letter codes, putting the letter just *before* in the alphabet, and then just *after*, and two before, and two after, and so on. Nothing makes sense."

Just then there was a series of beeps from Brendan's watch. It was an elaborate watch with lots of extra gadgetry on it.

"Is that a transatlantic phone call for you, Brendan?" Dessy grinned.

"If it's your alarm, you were planning to get up pretty late," said Molly.

113

"It's not the alarm," said Brendan. "That's off. It's a sound the watch has never made before."

He pressed some of the buttons around the side of the watch. Still the beeping sounds came, in a regular rhythm of one, two and three beeps: *Beep! Beep-Beep! Beep-Beep-Beep!*

"One beep, two beeps, three beeps, repeated and repeated," said Brendan. "What can it mean, and what's making the noise?"

Molly frowned and said: "You don't suppose it could be . . ."

"An extra message, like the one on the screen?" asked Brendan, wide-eyed.

Molly nodded. Dessy just said: "Wow!"

Brendan stared at the message, and said: "One, two, three. . . One, two, three. . ." Then he exclaimed: "Yes! That could be the clue to the code!"

"What do you mean?" Molly asked.

"Supposing for the first letter you jump one ahead in the alphabet, for the second letter two ahead, the third letter three, and then back to one again? And do that for each word in the message?"

"Good man, Brendan," said Dessy. "That's as clear as mud."

"Let me try it," said Brendan, ignoring him. "The first word is KMLJ. Suppose that means K plus one, which is the letter L, and M plus two, which is the letter O, and L plus three, another O, then back to plus one – J plus one, that's K. That makes the whole word, L-O-O-K. Look! We've cracked the code!"

"You're a wizard, Brendan!" said Dessy.

114

"A real genius," said Molly.

"With a little help from . . . a friend!" said Brendan. "Now let's get to work on the rest of the message. The second word is H plus one, that's I, then L plus two, that's N, so it spells *IN*."

Quickly he de-coded the complete message and wrote it down. "There it is!" he said. *"LOOK IN CURTAIN FOR ONES."*

"The curtain at the side of the stage!" said Molly, going across to it. "But what does it mean by *IN* curtain?"

"And what does it mean by *ONES?*" asked Dessy. "Shouldn't that be *FOR ONCE?* Whoever left the message can't spell, that's for sure."

"Don't be stupid," said Molly. "*ONES* must mean the Number One ballot papers. Now, *LOOK* IN *CURTAIN . . .*" She held up the corner of the curtain. The curtains had a lining fabric sewn on to the back of them. On the side, just near the bottom corner, Molly saw a tear where the sewing had come apart. She was able to reach her hand inside, between the curtain and its lining. "I think we've found the papers!" she cried.

Brendan and Dessy pressed round her excitedly, as she pulled out a square of paper. She held it out. The number 1 was written on it. She reached into the curtain and said: "I can feel a lot more papers in there."

"Let's get them all out!" said Brendan.

"Hang on," said Molly. "People might still say *we'd* planted them there. You stay here, and I'll go and get Emma Delaney, so she can take them out herself."

* * *

"That was smart detective work," said Emma as they pulled out the ballot papers and spread them on the table. "It was a real confidence trick. Barry Farrell must have gone backstage with another pad and scrawled a whole lot of Number Two papers, then switched them for these Number Ones."

They told her what they had seen at the racetrack.

"Well, he's certainly a clever crook," said Emma. "I never noticed anything during the ballot, any more than the people you saw at the racetrack did. And he wouldn't have needed that many switched papers to alter the score. It was 109 to 124. Now how many are there here?"

They counted 30 papers on the table. "That would be enough to make Number One the winners," said Molly, "and suppose he added twenty or so new Number Two's and we took them away from their score. . ."

"That would make it about 139 for Number One, against 104 for Number Two," said Brendan.

"Well," said Emma Delaney. "It looks like your festival plans can go ahead after all!"

* * *

"That's wonderful news!" said Joan Bright at the library. "It certainly doesn't give us much time, but we'll get busy at once."

"We've already got most of the pageant costumes done," said Molly.

"That's great," said Joan Bright, "and we can decorate the community hall with streamers and balloons, and hold the music and dance events in there."

"The Tug-of-War can be in the park below the castle," said Brendan, "and of course the grand finale will be in the castle itself, with Raven's concert."

"My dad could organise the fishing competition on the river, I'm sure," said Molly.

"And I'll judge the yo-yo competition," said Dessy. "Are judges allowed to compete as well?"

* * *

They e-mailed Billy Bantam saying they had got the go-ahead, and to thank him again for the funds he'd sent. He e-mailed back saying: *"Long Live the Ballygandon Festival! Wish I could be with you, gang.. Maybe next year, eh?"*

* * *

The Gang were in the grocery store one day, filling shelves, when Mrs O'Rourke came in. Luckily she didn't see them as they skulked out of sight behind the stacks, while she groused at Molly's mother and father.

"It's a put-up job!" she fumed. "That guard woman is in cahoots with the librarian and those children. Now we've got to abandon most of our plans. We'll still hold the casino and the poker competition, in Seamus's pub in Killbreen."

"I'm sure that will make a much better place for them," said Molly's mother coolly.

"By the way," said her father, "about the ticket money you've been collecting for Raven's concert. It would probably be simpler if Joan Bright took over the ticket sales now, and you handed over the money to her."

"She couldn't sell a ticket to a free dinner," sneered Mrs O'Rourke. "No, we'll keep control of that, and hand all the money over to charity as agreed."

"We'll have to make sure that really happens," Molly whispered to Brendan and Dessy.

"We will," said Brendan.

"Did you come in here to buy something, or just for a chat?" asked Molly's mother icily.

Mrs O'Rourke gave an angry snort, and marched out.

* * *

The festival drew big crowds to Ballygandon for all the events. Brendan won the fishing competition, and Dessy judged the yo-yo contest, and then gave a display of his own skills.

The Irish music and dancing got lots of competitors, and the musicians continued their playing at crowded sessions in the pub at night. As for the Tug-of-War, there had been rain during the night, and the heaving, sweating teams slipped and slithered, and most of the contests ended with both teams collapsed in the mud as the losers were pulled over the line.

Everyone congratulated Joan Bright and the Ballygandon Gang for making it a great success, and said the festival really should be held every year from now on.

"I can't believe it's all gone so smoothly," said Joan Bright, on the final day of the festival. They were just gathering everyone together in the field, ready for the pageant procession to go through the town. "Everyone's been really enthusiastic."

"Yes, even when Dessy fell in the river during the fishing, it didn't seem to frighten the fish," said Brendan.

"I tripped over your rod, that's what happened," said Dessy darkly.

"Never mind, it was good practice for your plunge in the pond today, as Horace O'Toole," said Molly.

"Trust me to get the sticky end of the lollipop," said Dessy.

"Come on, you've got a starring role," said Brendan, "*and* one of the best costumes."

Dessy was wearing a tall green, white and orange top hat, like the ones the Irish fans wear at matches. He had a thick black beard, and wore a flowing green cloak made out of an old flag.

Molly and Brendan were draped in sacks which they had painted in red and white stripes, and they were wearing the masks they had made from the halves of the old football. Molly had painted hers white with big red lips and green circles round the eyes. Brendan's was all blue and he thought it made him look like Braveheart in the movie. Molly had dressed Tina with a glittery red streamer tied round her neck.

In the procession there were donkey carts and ponies too, and Locky was sitting on a chair done up like a throne, in the back of Molly's father's pick-up truck. He had managed to borrow the red dressinggown with the fur collar from his friend in Horseshoe House, and had made a gold cardboard crown. He had stuck a black pointed beard on his chin, and was waving a large sword made out of a metal fence-post. Joan Bright wore a frilly old-fashioned gown and a red bonnet.

* * *

"Is everybody ready?" Locky called out through a megaphone.

"READY!" came the shout from everyone.

"Then let the Procession begin!"

At once the band struck up a rollicking tune, with Molly amongst them playing her tin whistle. In front of them at the head of the procession two boys carried a big banner painted with the words BALLYGANDON REVOLUTION! in big red letters.

Behind the band came a motley collection of costumed people, wearing everything from the sack cloaks and masks the gang had made, to sheets draped like Roman togas, and football shirts with sequins stuck all over them. Some marched, some skipped, and some even danced along. They waved sticks and balloons and even in one case a tennis racket. They were all laughing and giving whoops and whistles.

After them came a couple of jugglers flinging coloured balls in the air, two clown-costumed figures walking on tall stilts, and a man dressed like Charlie Chaplin, riding a unicycle.

Children of all ages whizzed along beside the procession on skates and scooters, cheering and catcalling.

Near the end came a donkey cart in which Dessy stood, wobbling a bit, and waving his fist in the air, chanting:

> *"Horace O'Toole!*
> *He's cruel, he's cool!*
> *Horace O'Toole makes the rules!"*

Finally there followed Molly's father's pick-up truck, with Locky being kingly on his throne, waving his sword and calling:

> *"Hullo, subjects, bow the knee!*
> *The Earl of Dunslaggin, that's me, me, me!"*

As the extraordinary procession went down the main street of Ballygandon, the footpaths were packed with people, laughing and cheering. The long line reached the end of the main street, then turned off on to the side-road that wound its way down towards the park just below the hill where the ruined castle towered above. They could see figures moving about in the ruins. They were Raven's roadies and stage managers, getting the castle courtyard ready for the big concert that evening.

The procession went through the park gates and across the grassy park until soon it came to the large pond which had a fountain in the middle with stone fish spouting water. The crowd gathered round the edge of the pond, until the donkey cart arrived and stopped. Dessy got out, and Locky got off his throne and climbed down from the pick-up truck. They were about to act out the dramatic highlight of the pageant, with the Earl of Dunslaggin proclaiming a knighthood for *Sir* Horace O'Toole. The costumed townspeople got ready to surge round Horace and throw him in the pond.

Dessy knelt down in front of Locky, who raised his sword in the air. But just then Molly cried out: "Hey! Look! Coming towards us!"

Everyone turned and saw approaching the gate one of Mrs O'Rourke's horse-drawn caravans.

"One of the holiday people must have decided to join the procession," said Joan Bright.

"If they have, they can't drive a caravan," said Molly. "Look how fast it's going, and it's swaying from side to side."

121

"It's heading straight across the park towards us," said Brendan. Then he shouted: "Scatter, everyone! That caravan's out of control!"

"And look who's driving it," said Dessy.

Visible now, standing on the platform and desperately trying to rein back the bucking horse, was Seamus Gallagher.

13

Triumph in the Ruins

The swaying caravan was coming straight for the crowd. People began rushing and stumbling to get out of the way.

Molly cried: "That horse is Rory!" Molly knew Rory well, and had sometimes ridden him bareback. They had even 'borrowed' him one night so that Molly could pretend to be the Phantom Horseman. Now she ran towards the approaching caravan.

"Stop, Rory, stop!" she shouted. She grabbed at Rory's bridle and tried to pull him up, but the horse went on charging forward, dragging her along. Suddenly Molly gave a great leap, and landed on Rory's back. She grasped the reins near where they joined the bridle, and she felt Seamus behind her let them go.

Molly tugged at the reins, calling: "Whoa, Rory, whoa!" She kept tugging hard on the reins so that the horse's head was pulled back. Rory snorted and neighed, but gradually slowed down. Finally he came to a stop just before the pond.

"Good boy, Rory, good boy," said Molly gently, as she stroked the horse's neck and the crowd cheered and clapped.

Seamus Gallagher had slumped down on the platform of the caravan. Now he stood up sheepishly and gazed at the scene. Then he peered around; he seemed to be looking for a way of escape.

"You shouldn't be driving a caravan if you can't control it!" said Joan Bright. They had never heard her speak so angrily before. "If it wasn't for Molly's courage, you could have crashed into the crowd. People might have been killed!"

There were some shouts and jeers of agreement from the spectators.

"My car broke down," said Seamus. "I had to get to a meeting in Killbreen."

There were more mutters of anger from the crowd, then cheers as Molly climbed down from Rory's back.

"Great girl, Molly!" said Dessy, as he helped her down.

"Thanks," said Molly, "and isn't Rory the great horse?" She stroked his neck.

"Well, I'd better get on," said Seamus. He reached behind him and produced a large brown tote-bag. He looked out at the crowd, and called: "Can anyone give me a lift into Killbreen?" He began nervously to climb down from the caravan.

"Why don't you walk, Seamus?" said Locky. "You could use the exercise!" There was laughter. Seamus scowled. Just then Molly's dog Tina, who had been wandering around among the crowd, came bounding across to Molly, barking happily.

"Hi, Tina!" said Molly.

But the barking alarmed Rory who began to rear up. Molly held tight to the reins and tried to calm the horse down, but his stamping and rearing shook the caravan and Seamus lost his footing on the step. He fell down right on top of Dessy who was standing not far from the edge of the pond. Dessy staggered backwards, clutching Seamus and trying to keep his own balance. He was right on the edge now, wobbling to and fro. Then suddenly with a cry he lost his balance altogether and fell backwards into the water, dragging Seamus with him. There was a great splash, and a roar of delight from the crowd as they watched the two figures floundering in the pond.

"Help! I can't swim!" yelled Seamus, spluttering and flapping his arms about.

Dessy stood up. The water was only waist-deep. "Try standing instead, you eejit!" he called.

Seamus stopped flapping and stood up unsteadily. Then he looked around in panic. "Where's my bag, where's my bag?" he shouted.

Dessy looked around too. Then he saw the brown tote-bag, floating in the water, about five metres away. He saw something else too. Several pieces of paper had come out of the bag and were floating on the pond. They looked very like banknotes.

Brendan had noticed them too. He pointed. "Look at that!" he cried. "Floating money!"

Molly said: "It looks as if Seamus must have been trying to run off with it. There must have been quite a lot in that bag."

"Hey!" said Brendan. "I reckon that could be the ticket money they collected for Raven's concert. He was probably going to meet Mrs O'Rourke and run away with it."

Seamus had seen the bag and the money too. Desperately he began to wade across the pond, flailing his arms. But Dessy was too quick for him. He launched himself forward and began to swim rapidly towards the bag. Brendan leaped in to help him.

Dessy grabbed the bag and held it high in the air. Brendan arrived and started to collect the floating banknotes.

"That's mine, that's mine!" Seamus shouted as he reached them, dripping and spluttering. He lunged at Dessy to try to grab the bag, but Dessy stepped back and he fell with a splosh on his face in the water.

He stood up, gasping, as Brendan said: "I've got them all, I think." He held up a wodge of sodden paper.

"Row for the shore, me hearties!" cried Dessy. He and Brendan waded for the bank, and miserably Seamus followed them, growling between splutters that the bag was his.

The crowd cheered again as Brendan and Dessy climbed out, and then helped Seamus to clamber on to the bank.

He stood there, soaking wet and glaring around him. Then he stared at Dessy, and said: "Just give me that, and I'll be on my way." He reached out for the bag.

"Not so fast!" said Dessy, turning away and opening the bag to see inside. "Look at that!" he went on, handing the bag to Locky.

Locky rummaged inside and said: "Wow, there's enough

cash in here for a prize for a horse-race! How did you come by this, Seamus?"

"And what's more, where were you taking it?" said Brendan.

"I bet he was going to meet Mrs O'Rourke. It's a hundred to one that that's the charity money from the tickets for Raven's concert."

"A good bet on a sure thing!" said Locky.

Seamus began to bluster and deny it, but they could see he was lying.

"Well, hello there!" They were all surprised to hear the voice of Raven, who had walked down the hill from the castle, and into the park. "What's going on? I saw a great kerfuffle happening down here, and decided to join in the fun."

"It's Seamus," said Molly. "He was bringing you the ticket money he collected for the charity concert this evening."

"Great, I was getting a bit concerned that he hadn't turned up with it yet," said Raven with some sarcasm.

Seamus began to mutter: "Well, it's not exactly. . . I mean to say. . ."

Raven interrupted: "Thanks a lot, Seamus. I'll take it now, shall I?" He stretched out his hand. Dessy handed him the bag. They saw Seamus's hand come up as if he was going to try to snatch the bag, but he thought better of it.

"Here's some more that escaped," grinned Brendan, holding out the damp wodge of notes.

"I've heard of *hot money* before, but I never heard of *wet money*," said Raven, taking it. "Well, I guess it will soon dry out."

Just then they heard a van coming across the park at some speed. It came to a stop just beside the caravan. Out stepped Mrs O'Rourke. "So this is where you got to!" she yelled, striding through the crowd towards Seamus. "When you didn't show up I came back and someone said you'd headed off in one of my caravans. Trying to skedaddle with my share of the money, were you?"

When she reached Seamus she suddenly saw Raven standing there too. She gasped. Seamus looked at her sourly and shrugged his shoulders.

"Hello, Mrs O'Rourke. How nice to see you," said Raven pleasantly. He held up the bag and the damp notes. "Seamus was good enough to bring me all the money you collected. He seems to have chosen a rather curious way to bring it, but anyway, here it is. Thank you both."

Seamus and Mrs O'Rourke just glared furiously at one another.

Another car drew up. This time it was a Garda car, and Emma Delaney and another guard got out of it. The crowd parted to let them through.

"Sorry to disturb the festival celebrations," said Emma with a smile. "But there've been some developments. We found that torch in the barn ruins, and we have certain fingerprint evidence too. So we would like you, Mr Gallagher, and Mrs O'Rourke too, to come to the station to help us with our inquiries. You might be able also to tell us where we can find Barry Farrell."

"No idea," said Seamus gruffly, as they were led off towards the Garda car. Brendan, standing just nearby, heard Seamus mutter to Mrs O'Rourke: "I haven't seen the swine since he sneaked off with our three-card-trick winnings on the day of the races."

As they all watched them go, Raven said: "Well, it looks like we could have two spare seats at the concert tonight."

"There's just one more ceremony I think I should perform!" cried Locky, raising his sword in the air. "Silence, please!" The noise of the crowd gradually subsided, as they all wondered what Locky was up to.

"Come here, would you, Dessy?" said Locky, and Dessy grinned and stepped forward.

Then Locky boomed in loud tones. "As the Earl of Dunslaggin, it is my decree that Horace O'Toole has today redeemed his reputation by saving the money – *and* by giving Seamus Gallagher a much needed bath!" There were cheers and laughs from the crowd. Locky went on: "I command you to kneel!"

"OK, Locky," Dessy grinned, kneeling. "I mean, OK, your Earlship."

Locky raised the sword and brought it down lightly first on Dessy's left shoulder and then on his right. He lifted up the sword again and proclaimed: "I now pronounce you *SIR Horace Dessy O'Toole!*"

Dessy stood up and clasped his hands above his head, as the shouts and cheers echoed across the park and the whole of Ballygandon.

* * *

It was getting dark as the audience began to gather in the castle for Raven's concert that night. There were rows of chairs set out in the big courtyard, and a platform in front of the gigantic old fireplace. Dim lights had been placed to show up the ruined arches and windows that loomed around the courtyard. There were spotlights to light up the stage, where the band's gear was already set up, and big loudspeakers at the side of the stage.

From their front row seats, the Ballygandon Gang, with Locky and Joan Bright, turned and gazed around them at the scene. There was an excited buzz from the audience.

"This must be like the kind of atmosphere there was here when they gathered for the big banquet on the night before Princess Ethna's wedding," said Molly.

"Let's hope tonight has a happier ending," said Dessy.

There was the sound of a regular, slow drum beating, as the lights began to dim. They saw the members of the band come in through an arch and make their way on to the stage. There was applause.

"I can't see Raven yet," said Brendan.

"He's probably going to fly in," said Dessy, staring up at the starry sky.

Just then the band played a dramatic fanfare, and all the lights went out. Soon they came up again, and there on the stage in a bright spotlight stood Raven, his headdress on and his black wings spread out. The audience cheered and clapped. Raven bowed, then reached for the microphone and began his first number.

* * *

The concert was a wild success, with the audience's

applause echoing round the ancient ruins after each song. When they came to the final song, Raven explained that he had composed this one specially for Princess Ethna who had met such a tragic fate here in this very castle all those centuries ago. He said he had been specially helped by Molly Donovan from Ballygandon, who would join in the accompaniment for the song on her tin whistle. He beckoned to Molly who climbed on to the stage to cheers and clapping and a piercing whistle from Dessy.

The haunting, melancholy song began. The only light was a single spotlight on Raven who sang the beautiful lilting melody with such power and feeling that many people felt the tears starting behind their eyes.

Brendan whispered to Dessy: "Listen, can you hear it?" He looked up, and so did Dessy, tilting his head.

"I think so," said Dessy. Accompanying Raven and the musicians there seemed to be another, high and wistful sound: a lovely distant voice, floating among the ruins, joining in.

At the end the audience stood and clapped for several minutes. When the applause finally died down, everyone stood in silent wonder. The faint voice in the sky seemed to be still singing the melody, far up among the ruined arches. Though the tune was a sad one, there was a feeling of happiness about the sound. Soon it began to fade, till finally there was only the deep silence of the night as the hushed crowds were still and the stars looked down from the sky on the castle of Ballygandon.

The End